Diana Philo lived and worked her early years in London, moving to Lincolnshire after her marriage.

These once alien, rural surroundings have become much loved, and she still lives there with her pet dachshund.

A Living To Die For

Diana Philo

A Living To Die For

Olympia Publishers
London

www.olympiapublishers.com
OLYMPIA PAPERBACK EDITION

Copyright © Diana Philo 2014

The right of Diana Philo to be identified as author of
this work has been asserted in accordance with sections 77 and 78 of the
Copyright, Designs and Patents Act 1988.

All Rights Reserved

No reproduction, copy or transmission of this publication
may be made without written permission.
No paragraph of this publication may be reproduced,
copied or transmitted save with the written permission of the publisher,
or in accordance with the provisions
of the Copyright Act 1956 (as amended).

Any person who commits any unauthorised act in relation to
this publication may be liable to criminal
prosecution and civil claims for damage.

A CIP catalogue record for this title is
available from the British Library.

ISBN: 978-1-84897-441-8

(Olympia Publishers is part of Ashwell Publishing Ltd)

This is a work of fiction.
Names, characters, places and incidents originate from the writer's
imagination. Any resemblance to actual persons, living or dead,
is purely coincidental.

First Published in 2014

Olympia Publishers
60 Cannon Street
London
EC4N 6NP

Printed in Great Britain

For Crispin, Piers, Candida, and Tarquin

1

Thomas drew the rough, grey blankets over his head and pulled up into the foetal position, knees against his chest and hands against his ears to shut out the world. His whole body ached but his back stung sharply from the beating. He focused on the hatred, gritting his teeth and grinding them together in the potency of it. He felt rather than heard his mother enter the attic bedroom. He knew that she suffered as much if not more than her children when his father was in drink but he could not contend with her pity and his own inadequacy to protect her or his siblings. He was eighteen, a man now. He told her to go away; that he didn't want her there. His voice sounded brutal even to him and he looked out from under the blankets to see her go out through the door, her back bent with the hurt that he knew was worse to her than any physical pain that she could suffer.

Sleep came to him despite himself. It was dawn when he awoke, the summer sun slanting through the small window low to the floor and casting a pool of yellow light on the bare boards. He heard the sounds of the farm coming to life; the noises he had grown up with. The soft mooing of the cows in the byre and the scratching and clucking of the hens about their morning business. The flapping of wings as the geese preened themselves in the morning sun by the pond and of old Dexter, the carthorse as his hooves moved restlessly on the brick floor of his stable, eager to be off.

Thomas lay still, listening for the latch on the kitchen door to rattle. His father would have taken his porridge in silence while his mother had learned long ago to speak only when she was spoken to, so no sound came up the wooden staircase until the scraping of his chair on the stone floor heralded his father's readiness to leave. Thomas imagined the scene. His father would turn to the hook on the wall by the door and take down his cap, place it squarely upon his head and, with the scarf knotted round his neck where it became white in contrast to the ruddiness of his weathered face, he would turn and stare at his wife and she back at him. Without a word he would unlatch the door and leave. Alice Blackwell would look at the place where he had been then sink into a chair, her head in her hands.

William, the youngest by four years, would be first down and still unable to stem his eagerness for the day ahead in the resilient way of the young, would sit at the table spoon in hand, waiting for his porridge. Amy, their fifteen year old sister would be last down, crawling reluctantly from her bed in the attic, rubbing the sleep from her eyes and pulling at her tousled red hair, the colour of the copper kettle on the hob.

Thomas remembered her as a little tot, pretty as a picture with her ivory skin and pink cheeks, full of spirit, her little chubby legs scrambling to keep up with him as they played in the hay loft while the sun slanted through the cracks between the boards and caught her fiery hair in its flaming sunbeams. Now she was beginning to follow her mother's way and keep her own council. Her smile was so seldom an occurrence that Thomas would hold on to it for as long as it lasted, a speck of sunlight in this dour place.

He raised himself painfully to a sitting position and swung his legs to the floor. He splashed his face with water from the ewer and ran his fingers through his thick head of dark hair, then pulled the rough shirt and jersey over it and down over his sore ribs, covering the purple and blue marks. Trousers on and belted, he pushed his bare feet into the leather boots and clattered down the stairs to the kitchen. His mother glanced up from the saucepan on the fire where she stirred the porridge. William was engrossed in his noisy eating. Thomas sat down at the table and his mother placed a bowl in front of him, her eyes questioning him.

'You'll be late for your work this morning.'

'I'm not going.' He saw his mother stop in her tracks but he continued to spoon the thin porridge into his mouth.

*

Amy lay in bed listening for her father's coughing outside the back door. Each morning he would clear the phlegm from his throat before striding over to the stable, kicking the chooks out of the way as he went. He was not a tall man but stocky, the upper part of his body well developed by the work that he did. His hair was the red he had passed on to his daughter but straight and mussed from the dust in it. Even his thick brows and lashes were red, lost in the ruddiness of his complexion. But the stubble that covered his jutting chin was blue-black and would have been dark auburn had it been allowed to grow into a beard. Traces of the handsome youth he had once been survived but two missing teeth and the unpleasant set of his mouth gave him a look of antagonism that kept men at arm's length.

It was the same each morning now, the relief that he was away all day and they could all breathe freely; go about their lives but with the knowledge that evening would bring him back perhaps quiet and brooding, perhaps raging and banging his fist or worse, stripping his thick leather belt from his trousers and threatening his wife and sons. He didn't threaten her. Oh no! He had a different agenda for Amy. His mood then would be pleasant and amiable, fawning and obsequious; the mood they all feared worst. He would send them all to bed early. All except Amy. He would take the bottle from the dresser and pour a small glass for Amy and a large one for himself. It was useless for her to refuse the colourless liquid and he would pull back her head by her red hair, his red hair, and force it down her throat. Then he would take his own drink and the neat gin must barely touch his throat on its way to join the rest that already lined his stomach.

Last evening had been one such night. He had returned from the public house in the village with glazed eyes and a leering smile that stretched from ear to ruddied ear. He had staggered to the table drawing out his chair and demanding his meal. The food was near cold and his mood had at once changed to that of uncontrolled anger. He had picked up the bowl and flung it at his wife catching her a glancing blow on the forehead, as the contents streamed down her face and chest. Thomas had leapt to her defence and received a vicious beating for his trouble; a beating which seemed to soak up all the pent up anger in her father so that he sat then twisting the leather belt between his thumbs and fingers and catching his breath. Then the drooling smile returned as he turned his attention to Amy.

What followed was a blur in Amy's mind for she would shut down and think of other things: of the boy in the town with the corn-coloured hair who winked at her from behind the stall in the market place or of the beautiful yellow dress with the frills in the window of the dress-maker's shop. If she concentrated hard and didn't fight it would not take long and her father would pull away, pushing her aside like a rag doll and sink into the chair beside the fire. He would light his pipe and she would creep upstairs and cry into her pillow until sleep released her.

Across the attic, in the next room, William would listen to his sister's crying. He didn't know why she cried. Perhaps it was because Thomas had received such a vicious beating. He, William, had hidden under the table while it had transpired. He had learned long ago to use his legs and find some place where his father could not find him when he had a rage on him. He wondered why Thomas did not do the same instead of wading in and getting involved. He didn't like it when his mother had bruises and cried. He wished she would come with him and hide in the barn or in the chicken coop and wait until his father slept by the fire, snoring his head off. At least now it would be quiet for a few days, he thought and fell asleep.

At midday father came back looking for Thomas, demanding to know why he had not been in the fields where he was needed at hay-making. Mother sat at the table crying into her apron and Amy beside her, her own eyes red with weeping.

'What ails you both? Give up that snivelling,' the man demanded.

'Tom has gone,' screamed Amy, 'and we shall never see him again!'

'Gone? Where has he gone to?'

'Thomas has gone to enlist in the army,' said mother, standing up and staring her husband in the face, undaunted and resolute at this time despite Fred Blackwell's growing anger.

'Thomas has gone to the army and he will be killed and it will be your fault!' cried Amy shaking her clenched fist at him. He drew back his hand and slapped her across the face, sending her reeling against the dresser. The plates on the shelves shivered then lost their balance and fell to the floor where they broke on the stones into shards round her feet. His chin jutting out and his eyes wide, he caught her by her bodice and thrust his rough face close to hers but the look that she gave back to him could have turned him to dust. She snatched free and went out through the door to run up to the copse and cry out her heart.

William clung to his mother's skirts. It was too late to run, for his father never normally returned before nightfall and he was between him and the door. His father slumped into his chair, silent now and mother loosened William's hold on her skirt and went upstairs to her room.

Two days and nights went by and Fred Blackwell never moved from his chair except to piss in the grass outside the door. Mother went about her chores around him, laid food on the table that was hardly touched then cleared it away mechanically. On the third morning he rose and put on his cap and scarf and without a word left the house for the fields. They heard him fetch Dexter from his stall and the big horse's hooves on the cobbles echoed across the silent yard.

2

At nightfall, father returned full of drink. He sat without speaking and ate the rabbit stew that was put before him, tearing a hunk of bread from the loaf at his side and scraping his plate clean with it. He sent mother and William to their beds catching Amy by the arm to restrain her, and banged the gin bottle down upon the table. This time Amy wrestled and fought hard to push him off. She succeeded, for the drink made him slow this night. She dashed for the door but he stepped in front and barred the way drawing the leather belt from his trousers. Amy in her turn, ran around the table until it was between her and her father, grabbing the bread knife and holding it aloft, daring him to approach her. Her father stared through watery eyes, swaying from side to side. He suddenly threw back his head and laughed, a deep throated sound gurgling in his craw then without warning and with surprising swiftness, he rounded the table towards her. At that same moment Amy struck, plunging the bread knife into his chest with all the strength in her young body. All the hatred she had harboured she felt then rising from her stomach, swelling up into her chest, pulsing up into her shoulders and arms and the extraordinary strength of it. She stared into his reddened face as the shock struck him. She watched his eyes open wide and his jaw drop soundlessly but his outstretched hand did not leave her bodice. She pulled back and struck again and the blade went into the muscle of his arm-pit and then again she drove the knife into his stomach with surprising ease. And she left it there. His eyes stared unbelieving at her as he crumpled against the table then staggered to his chair clutching the knife that was still embedded in his body. Amy was frozen now, her eyes unable to leave him. He looked down at the knife and then again at her, his eyes boring into hers before falling forward into the ashes of the grate.

Amy stood looking at the body of her father for a long time, unable to move. Then she found her voice at last and screamed for her mother. Mother came down the stairs in her nightgown, a shawl hastily draped round her shoulders. William was behind her, bleary eyed from sleep. When she saw the body of her husband lying in the cinders, she clasped her hands to her mouth calling for God to forgive them all.

'Is he dead?' she whispered.

'Aye and I'm glad of it. He will not push his filthy body into mine again nor will he beat you senseless. I wish I'd have done it long ago and perhaps we would have Tom with us now.' Amy said defiantly.

'What will become of us? Oh, God Almighty what have you done Amy?'

'Say you're glad of it mother. At least say that.'

'Oh God the Father,' was all she got in return.

They sat in the kitchen with the body face down in the ashes at their feet. William tugged at his mother's nightgown demanding to know why his father lay there, not understanding. At last the silence was broken and Amy said, 'shall I go for the magistrate?' Her mother darted her a frightened look.

'No girl, no. I cannot lose you too. I *will* not lose you.' And then, 'William, go to your room and stay until I tell you. We must see to your father.'

William protested. 'Why is he lying there? Is he drunk again? Will you get him up?' She pushed him gently towards the stairs. 'And close the door behind you... and the curtains.' When he had gone and they heard the door close Amy looked questioningly at her mother.

'We will get rid of the body,' said her mother.

'But where? And what shall we say to folks?'

'We will say he has gone looking for Tom... gone after him to fetch him back. We'll weight the body and put it in the marsh. It will never be found. Horses and cattle have disappeared into that bog with no trace.'

'Mother the marsh is more than a mile from here. He... it is too heavy even with the two of us.'

'Hush child, let me think.'

Amy had not noticed in the dark kitchen that her clothes were damp with blood. She leapt up, disgusted, pulling her clothes away from her skin. Her hands and her arms too were bloodied. She rushed over to the pump to wash them.

'Leave it!' shouted her mother. 'There will be more blood before the night is out.' Amy began to sob uncontrollably and her voice rose into hysteria as she tugged at her clothes to rid herself of the stained fabric of her skirt and bodice. Her mother rose and clutched her shoulders with firm hands.

'Hush girl. I cannot do this alone.' Amy stopped crying at once, surprised at her mother's sudden and unaccustomed strength of will. Alice Blackwell paced the floor, her hand to her forehead then swung round to Amy.

'It will start to get light in two hours. We have no time to lose. There is a barrow in the barn. Go and fetch it. Go! Now!' When Amy returned with the wooden barrow, the back door was open and her mother had wrapped the body in a blanket and tied it with string round the neck and legs. She was breathless with the effort and stood leaning on the edge of the table, her face white and drawn, her eyes closed in concentration.

'Mother. Are you all right?'

'Help me get this into the barrow,' she said, ignoring Amy's question. The blanket was already stained in blood and where the body had lain was a pool that the ashes had soaked up, already dry. It took all the strength of the two women to wrestle the body onto the barrow. At one point, the blanket came adrift and the ghastly face stared up at them both with wild dead eyes. Amy shrieked and sprang back in horror dropping the legs she had been lifting. The body rolled onto the floor as if it desired to return to its place in the ashes. Amy's mother hastily covered the face and retied the string tightly around the neck. Amy wanted to cry out that she would strangle him if she tied it too tightly and felt laughter rising in her throat at the absurd thought. When they had settled the body in the barrow, mother went out to look up at William's window to make sure that the curtains were drawn. It was still dark but a thin line of white marked the horizon and the first light of day.

They began the interminable journey, the metal wheel of the barrow resisting each large stone or clump of grass they came to. They were forced to rest often and Amy glanced back over her shoulder at the encroaching dawn. A heavy mist rose from the marshland ahead and a soft wind played it into patterns. It was almost palpable in its resemblance to a fine gauze or muslin fabric and parted like a curtain, falling back into place once they had passed through it. Amy shivered and she saw the blanket on the body in the cart had droplets of dew on its surface.

'Not far now,' said her mother, sensing her anxiety. The ground had become softer and the barrow unmanageable. 'We will have to drag it from here.' Amy shrank back.

'I can't touch it any more, mother. I can't, I can't.' Her mother ignored her and pulled the head end off the barrow.

'Take the legs, Amy,' she commanded, 'and watch where you put your feet.' She knew the nature of land where she had been born and raised, that assumed a solid base where none existed and they dragged the body or rolled it in front of them. Mother put up her hand to stop and peered into the mist at the marsh ahead.

'Mind where you put your feet there,' she said again. Then, 'Stay back, Amy.' She went on alone treading carefully and peering first at the types of grasses that indicated a firm foot hold. She paused, then turned and came back to where Amy stood staring down at the wrapped body of her father, unable to tear her eyes from it. Her mother was carrying a large flat stone she had picked up on the way. She untied the ropes and rolled the body out from the blanket then placing the stone on the chest, picked up a stout branch and used it to lever the body to the left of where they stood. It appeared to Amy to float but prone and unmoving it did not at once sink, for it is often the struggling and desperate need to be upright of a living being that sucks a body down. Mother used the stick to push down on the body and bubbles began to explode around it as she forced it into the porridge-like substance. When Amy turned back to look, it was gone and the surface was quiet once more, the mist swirling back into place over it. They waited, staring at the place where he had been, half expecting him to rise up again with those dead, staring eyes. Mother came to first and rubbed her hands on her apron and took hold of Amy by the shoulders.

'Come now. We must get back for it will break dawn soon. We are not done yet.'

'Can't we sink the barrow too?' said Amy.

'No child. We shall have need of it. We shall have to run the farm on our own from now on.'

Dawn was breaking as they arrived back at the kitchen door.

'Now, I will make us a hot drink while you go take off those clothes and wash yourself. Look in on William and leave him if he is asleep. We have yet to deal with him.' When Amy came back down to the kitchen, her mother was scrubbing the floor by the fireplace and two steaming mugs were set on the table.

'Drink and rest. Is William asleep still?'

'Yes mother.'

'When you have done, put those clothes in the tub to soak.' When they had between them eradicated all signs of the night's activities, mother sat down opposite Amy at the table. Amy's arms were red from scrubbing them with soap and ice cold water, over and over, to cleanse them.

'You must get over this terrible happening, Amy or it will ruin your life. He was a bad man through and through and only you were strong enough to stop him. If I had had your strength, I would have done the same a long time ago. I wish for your sake that it had been me. There is not a soul in this district who will mourn his going. You were only defending yourself. Listen to me Amy!' Amy started and focused on her mother now.

'What will we tell William?'

'We will say that his father had just lost consciousness and that we dressed his wounds from the fall and that he went out early this morning to fetch Thomas back. We shall have to act normal for his sake. There has been enough suffering under this roof and it is time it stopped. Our time will be taken up with trying to run this place alone for it is our only living. It will not come easy for two women, Amy.'

'I will do a man's work, mother. I know I can.'

'Then that's settled. I will make breakfast and you will call William when it is ready, for the sooner we get our story into his young head, the better.' She turned her attention to the fire and when the flames were curling strongly round the black porringer, she stepped over to the hook by the door, took down Fred Blackwell's cap and scarf and plunged them into the burning flames.

3

In the following weeks the work was hard and the hours long. When the neighbours heard of Thomas leaving to join the army and his father following to fetch him back, they were not surprised in either case. That Thomas had stayed under the same roof for so long was a wonder but that his father was prepared to leave two women to look after the farm alone, a typical act of the man they knew. For their sakes and not for his, they helped out whenever possible but times were lean and with their own farms to tend, there was little they could do.

    The Blackwell farm was well placed and sat upon some of the most fertile land in the district. It spread alongside the marsh from which the goodness leached. By the time it had reached the neighbouring farms it was spent and had nothing left to give. The marsh had its own climate that held the moisture under each evening's blanket of mist and saved the farmland from drying out when the rains were long in coming. Previous generations of Blackwells had dug dykes to bring the excess water down from the marsh to feed a pond from which the water was brackish to the taste but clear and clean. The farmhouse itself was like many others of its kind, in which generations born and bred to the life would spend it there until they turned up their toes to make room for the next. Built of stone in the main, the steeply pitched roof housed the three attic bedrooms set above the kitchen and parlour. The roof extended to cover a hayloft and open stabling to house animals below. The only chimney was built of small brick and stretched up one end of the building narrowing on its way to tower above the roof tiles by six feet or so. The small windows were polished clean and neatly curtained and the low hedges either side of the only door were clipped for the washing to be spread to dry in the wind and fade in the sun.

Alice Blackwell had been fifteen when she had come to the farm as a bride with little recollection of her life before it. It seemed to her as though she had always been there. She was one of thirteen children and had scant memory of her mother who had died giving birth to the thirteenth child, used up like an autumn leaf fallen from the tree. Alice had mothered her five youngest siblings so had taken easily to motherhood though the brutality with which her own children had been conceived had come as a fearful shock to her. In some ways it had been fortunate that her husband drank so much that he was so often unfit for anything but to snore in their bed until morning. But she was not to foresee that with the drink would come later, violence, not just towards her but to their children also.

*

When Amy found herself to be with child, she didn't tell her mother immediately for she knew that she would try to lessen Amy's load and take on more herself. The burden was so great that it occupied Amy's every waking hour. Harvest was approaching and how could she do a man's work when she became heavy with child? What would they tell their neighbours who were all rallying round to help the two women but would no doubt judge her a loose woman, unmarried as she was? Who could she say was the father when it was demanded of her? They would certainly have no more to do with such a family. It was all so terrible. She longed for Thomas and missed him so much, the only light in her short life, the only one who had brought any laughter to her. And they *had* laughed – she and Tom, when they were children. William was a sulky child and too young to understand any of this, so it must be kept from him. Her mother was already bent under the worry of the farm. And what of her father? She had killed him in cold blood and he lay now in the dank wetness of the bog not a mile from where she spent her days. She could not get him out of her mind and he rose up from his watery grave in the night when she tried to sleep, his eyes black sockets but still able to follow her movements; his gnarled hands still able to clutch at her clothes.

More than two months had gone by and Amy kept her secret but her mother, guessing that her morning ague was more than tiredness and the pressure of work, confronted her. Amy felt some relief in telling her.

'There can be no more lies, Amy. We have been forced to sin enough for one lifetime.'

'But mother, we cannot tell folk what really happened. You cannot manage here alone and with a baby to bring up. Mother, I don't want to die. I don't want to die.' Amy sobbed into her mother's shoulder.

'Hush child. What's done is done and in the past. We have learned to live with it but from now on we live like honest folk. We shall go to the parson and tell him about your father and what he was like; what he did. People hereabouts knew him to be a drinker and quick with his fists. The parson will not find it hard to believe that he abused his own daughter. We say not that he is dead but that he went away, that we are glad and that we hope he never comes back. Our last untruth for I won't lose you for the sins of your father. He will advise us. Go fetch your shawl and bring mine. We'll go now, at once.'

4

It was still early morning for those that were not farming folk when they knocked on the door of the parsonage. The house was across the cemetery from the church and a late summer mist still lay heavy over the moss-covered grave stones as the two women stood waiting for their knock on the heavy oak door to be answered. A watery sun sent slanting rays onto a carved angel poised with outspread wings above a family grave and seemed to look at Amy and her mother with sad, stone eyes. Dark green ivy glistening with dew clung to its feet and clutched at the stony legs as if to prevent the angel from flying away. A girl of about Amy's age opened the door and made a little curtsy.

'Why Amy, it's you,' she said. 'I haven't seen you for a long time. Is it the parson you want? For he's out over in the church saying morning prayers. He'll be back soon. Sit here in the hall Mrs Blackwell for he won't be long to be sure. Now I have to go about my duties you understand.' The girl hurried away to the kitchen and they were left in the dark wood panelled hall. A heavy coat hung on the hook and walking sticks with a variety of carved heads stood in a rack beside the door. A well worn mat ran the length of the hallway and several closed doors concealed rooms off it. A large aspidistra in a copper pot stood on a tall stand at the base of a wooden uncarpeted staircase and coloured rays of autumn morning light shone on the stairs from a stained glass window half way up the flight. The two women did not speak for the environment did not encourage it.

At last, they heard footsteps on the gravel path outside and the parson opened the door, taking off his broad-brimmed hat as he entered and hanging it above the coat. He was a rotund figure with short, curved and muscular stockinged legs beneath his tight breeches. He was in the habit of folding his hands across his stomach and resting them there since they hardly reached the pockets of his long frock coat.

'Well, well, who have we here?' he said in a parsonical voice. 'Come into the morning room. Come. Come,' he urged them, shuffling them before him through the door of a spacious room in which a large table was laid for breakfast. Alongside was a pile of books which seemed to have spilled from the lines of book shelves near it, some lying open from recent use. He sat down and beckoned them to sit opposite him. 'You will not object to me taking some refreshment? It is my habit to go over to the church on waking and offer my devotions before I break my fast.' He did not wait for a reply but tucked a napkin into his collar and rang a small bell on the table beside him. The girl, Emily, who had answered the door to them came in with a tray and the parson set to on the cold lamb and fresh baked bread set before him. 'Now what help can I be to you, Mrs Blackwell and – Amy is it?' he said at last. Amy's mother was brief and to the point with the chosen pieces of her story and the parson was forced to put down his knife and fork, his cheeks becoming even pinker, if that were possible as the story came to its unfortunate climax.

'My dear lady, I had heard of your husband's character but this, this is monstrous,' he said, wiping his mouth vigorously with the napkin. 'What are we to do? What indeed! I feel the need for a medicinal brandy. Will you join me Mrs Blackwell?' He walked over to the tray table beside the window and poured himself a generous brandy from the flagon, assuming Mrs Blackwell's refusal rather than waiting for it. 'We have a predicament here. Indeed, a predicament. Not only have we a child to be born out of wedlock, but the... child... of... I'm not sure there is a word for it, Mrs Blackwell, and if there is I have no knowledge of it. You have indeed been through hard times ladies and more to come, more to come it seems. I cannot blame you for celebrating his departure and I think the blackguard would do well to stay away but I hardly think he will show his face again, eh? But this deliberation is hardly solving the problem.' The parson paced the room for a while, swirling the brandy in his glass and studying it as he murmured under his breath and finally downing the liquid in one gulp.

'Have you a beau, Amy?' he asked at last. 'Someone of whom you are fond, perhaps?'

'No sir,' she said.

'It is my belief that an urgent and immediate marriage would solve a number of your problems, my dear. Is there no one?'

Amy looked flustered.

'She has worked hard and long hours on the farm since a young girl and she is barely turned sixteen. There has been little time for romance in her young life,' said her mother catching hold of her hand. 'She has been a good and loyal daughter and borne her troubles with fortitude.'

'Yes, yes of course, Mrs Blackwell but someone must be found. Amy is a handsome girl to be sure and the farm is an attractive proposition to a young man... ' he trailed off in his thoughts and then, 'Amy, this is not every young woman's dream of courtship and marriage and how it should come about. Are you prepared to take on a man of my choice to preserve the honour of you and your family and give a name to your unborn child?'

'I suppose… ' Amy glanced at her mother who continued to stare at the floor. 'Yes, sir. I am.'

'Good girl, good girl. Now it only remains for me to find the young man.' The parson turned from his perambulations and held out his hand indicating the conclusion of their business. 'I shall be in touch, ladies. I shall be in touch.'

When they arrived back at the farm, William was feeding the chooks with a disgruntled look on his face.

'I'm fair starving,' he said. 'You've been a long while.'

Over their porridge, mother explained that they had been to see the parson and that Amy was to marry. She didn't mention the expected child. He did not need to know that.

'Who is she to marry?' he said.

'The parson is to choose a suitable young man.'

'But what will father say when he comes back?'

'He may not come back… for a very long time and we have the farm to run. You must understand that he may never come back William.'

'But then the farm falls to Tom and me, not some stranger.' He did not appear too concerned that his father may never return.

'The farm will always be Tom's and yours first, Will. Never fear. But we cannot afford hired help and we must do something.'

'I will *not* like him and he will *not* tell me what I must do for I will be in charge until Tom comes back.' William pushed his bowl away from him, got up and flung out of the door.

'There is something of his father in that boy but he'll come round,' said mother.

'*He* doesn't have to like him. It is I who will have to share my bed with him for the rest of my life, to look at him across the table and wash his undergarments.' Amy burst into tears. Her mother went to her and put her arms around her.

'Amy, he may be a nice boy, have you thought of that? Don't think the worst until the worst happens. All men are not as your father was. Think of Thomas. A kinder and more pleasant young man there never was. I'm sure the good parson will not choose unwisely.'

5

A week went by and then another when, as they were seated at the table for the evening meal, there was a knock on the door, then the latch was lifted and the parson entered. He was accompanied by a tall willowy man who appeared to be in his late twenties. He took off his cap and stood just behind the parson and would have been concealed by him had not the reverent gentleman been a head shorter than him.

'Mrs Blackwell. Amy. William,' acknowledged the parson placing his broad-brimmed hat on the table. 'I have brought along a young man to meet you Amy. He is of good character and from the village of Westbury where he farms with his two brothers. He has been married before but sadly his wife and child were lost to this world at the birth. He understands your condition, Amy, but is prepared to take on the child as his own.' Mother glanced at William but he was busy in a sulk and went on eating his meal. She raised her eyebrows in a sign to the parson and then at William and the parson nodded his understanding that he would not speak freely in front of the boy. He reached out and took the man's arm, drawing him forward into the light of the candles. He was neither unpleasant nor handsome in the face with dark brown eyes that seemed kindly enough. His hair was dark and somewhat tousled and his face ruddy from the fields but his clothes were clean enough and he seemed to have made some effort in his dress. He fingered his hat in his hands, turning it over and over with apparent nervousness.

'Your name and age, young man?' asked mother. The man cleared his throat.

'I am Charles Edwin Marriot and my age is thirty four, Mrs…'

'Blackwell, man. I told you, Blackwell,' interrupted the parson with some irritation.

'He is nigh on twenty years her senior, parson,' said Alice Blackwell. The parson moved closer to her and spoke quietly into her ear.

'My dear lady, I'm sure the age difference will be of no consequence. You must know how difficult it has been to find a suitable husband for Amy in her present condition. It is not many men who are prepared to take on another man's child as his own and keep his council on it. The only other was in his late forties and already with the gout.'

'Now Amy – Charles, what do you think on it?' he said, standing up and facing them both. The candidates stood with downcast eyes, facing each other but neither spoke. 'Come, come now. Surely you have an opinion?' said the parson impatiently. Eventually, Amy spoke in a small voice.

'He looks kindly enough.'

'Good. Good. Charles?'

'She is a fine-looking girl and no mistake,' volunteered Charles, his cheeks flaming.

'Then that is settled. Can we assume your blessing on their courtship, Mrs Blackwell?'

'Amy?' said her mother. Amy nodded and sat down at her place at the table.

'Good, good,' said the parson again, rubbing his hands together. 'Now the courtship will be necessarily brief and so I will read the bands at church service on Sunday evensong and have the vicar of Westbury do likewise. Splendid, splendid.' William, having finished his meal pushed back his stool and left the room without a backward glance, a black expression on his face. The parson appeared not to notice his rudeness.

'I will go now and leave these two young people to begin to get to know each other. I have every confidence in this union Mrs Blackwell every confidence and I'm sure that Charles will be an asset to you here on the farm. A boon, a boon, I'm sure.' With that, the parson donned his hat and took his leave. Charles remained standing and playing with his hat while Amy sat staring at her now cold meal.

After a lengthy silence, Mother said,

'Perhaps you two would like to take a walk to the pond. It's a fine evening but will be dark soon. Take your shawl, Amy for it's growing chilly in the evening these days. I shall have a hot drink ready when you come back.' Amy rose from the table and still with eyes averted, put her shawl round her shoulders. Charles lunged forward in a clumsy attempt to help her but missed his chance as she made for the door. He followed her, placing his hat on his head and closing the door behind them.

The air was chilled and Amy drew her shawl about her shoulders. The branches of the trees were heavy with the rain that had fallen earlier and grey clouds filled the darkening sky promising more rain to come in the night. The track was dotted with puddles that reflected the forbidding clouds above and they were forced to pick their way between them. They walked in silence, Amy leading the way and Charles two paces behind. He drew forward.

'May I call you Amy, Miss Blackwell? They call me Charlie at home.' She shrugged and walked on and then she said,

'The parson said you'd been married before.'

'Yes,' he said simply.

'Did you love her?'

'She was my cousin,' he replied.

'But did you love her?' insisted Amy stopping to look at him.

'I suppose. It was always understood from when we were children.'

'Will you love me?' said Amy staring into his face

'You are certainly very pretty,' he answered after a moment's pause.

'That is not what I asked.'

'But I don't know you yet. Er... I look forward to getting to know you,' he said nervously. Amy thought for a moment as if considering a reply.

'When we marry you must sleep away from me. I will not have you touch me. Do you understand?'

'You are with child. I understand.'

'It is not the child,' she said and started back towards the house leaving him standing looking after her. 'You'd better come back for mother will expect us both,' she said without turning round.

6

'What brought you to the vicarage, Amy, the other day?' said Emily, tripping alongside Amy and holding up her Sunday dress to save it from the muddy path. Amy hesitated. She had to gather her thoughts to settle on how much to tell her friend. She concentrated on the ground, picking her way between the puddles from the rains the night before to give herself time to think.

'I am to be married,' she said shortly.

'Oh Amy, how excellent. And who is the lucky young man? Do I know him? How long has he been courting you? When is the wedding to take place? And…'

Amy held up her hand to stop her friend. 'To which of all these questions do you wish me to reply first, Emily, because I'm sure I have forgot the first one while thinking about the last. You do not know him as he is from the other side of Westbury where he farms. His name is Charles Edwin Marriot. Will that do?'

'It is just a beginning Amy. How did you meet him?' Amy was stopped in her tracks for she had given no thought to the answer to that question. She pretended to smooth her skirt and pick off an imaginary speck of dirt, and then, 'My brother Tom brought him to supper one night.' Fairly satisfied with her reply, Amy strode off along the track.

'But how did it progress from there, Amy? At what point did you fall in love and when did he propose marriage? What did it feel like, no, what does it feel like to be in love?' Emily stood staring up into the branches of the trees that lined the track in a daze of romantic imaginings.

'Oh come on Emily. We shall never get to market at this rate or if we do, everything will have been sold and the stalls empty,' said Amy irritably, striding on ahead.

'You don't seem very happy about it,' sulked Emily running to catch up with her.

The track became broader as it neared the small market town and was surfaced with gravel and edged with stones to prevent carts from going off the path and sinking into the soft verges. The small stones felt sharp through the worn soles of Amy's boots but at least the mud was less of a problem. As the girls approached the market, the sounds of voices grew louder; the calls of street vendors describing their wares and of greetings and laughter as friends met who had not seen each other for many months. The inn was doing a roaring trade and men spilled out onto the cobblestones, slopping their ale as they pushed each other to find a bench to sit down on after a long walk or a longer ride. Animal and bird calls laced through the human voices to make up an amalgam of sound that was both buoyant and a little alarming at the same time. The girls were used to the quiet of the countryside and the bustle and smell of so many people gathered together was bewildering. Emily hung on to a piece of Amy's shawl, desperate in case they should be separated by the throng. Amy pushed on through the crowd, holding her basket in front to shield her chest from elbowing men.

'Where are we going?' asked Emily.

'I have a friend I wanted to see,' said Amy stretching to see over the heads of people nearby to see if the boy with the corn-coloured hair was on his stall today. She didn't know what she would say if he were there or even why she was looking for him since she was now betrothed to an old man, pregnant and her life ruined. He was not there and she could not credit her disappointment. What had she thought? That he would whisk her away to a place were her pregnancy could be undone and shelter her in a little cottage surrounded by flowers and perpetual blue skies? 'Don't be ridiculous Amy,' she said to herself.

'What did you say Amy?' asked Emily trying hard to keep up. Amy didn't bother to reply but pressed on to the ribbon stall to get the things her mother had asked for for the baby clothes that she was proposing to make. Further on Amy stopped.

'Emily, why do you not go to the stalls that you need for your purchases and we shall meet later at the butter cross? That way we may get home before darkness falls. I do not relish picking my way through puddles with just the moonlight to guide me.' Emily agreed reluctantly. Amy did not want her to see the purchases she was about to make for there would be more questions and Amy was tired to death of thinking of answers.

As she wandered through the market having made her purchases, she met a boy with whom she had been at school. They had never been friends but Amy wished to ask him about the corn-haired boy so she feigned an interest in his life since leaving the little school house. Finally, she was able to ask her question and was told that the corn-haired boy had done as Thomas had probably done and enlisted as a pikeman in Cromwell's army. Amy asked about the roll of a pikeman and the boy explained that they were engaged in protecting the musketeers, two pikemen to each because the muskets took so long to load and the musketeers were vulnerable while priming their weapons. Amy was not sure that she understood but she had heard enough and took her leave. She bought some cold apple pie on the way to meet Emily at the cross in the centre of the market square and sat waiting for her on the steps, munching the pie.

At last Emily turned up, her basket cheeping sweetly from the chicks she had stowed in it. She lifted the corner of the cloth that covered it and Amy peeped in at the tiny yellow creatures and the startled brown hen that crouched there, its red eyes darting at the sudden light.

'I know that my mother will be pleased. It is very late in the year for chicks so I had no hope to find any.'

'They are so lovely Emily but have you not enough chickens to make your own?'

'The fox took the lot the other night and we were left with but two cockerels and a single duck; bodies and feathers everywhere. It was a massacre to be sure.'

'Have you eaten anything Emily for we should start for home soon?'

'I had a beef patty soon after I left you and a swig of my friend's ale when I passed the inn. My money was all gone by then and I was glad to see her there outside.'

'Come on then. We shall start back and with any luck, be back before that rain cloud,' Amy pointed up at the sky at a looming cumulus cloud suspended in a glowering background of grey, 'empties its rain on our heads and soaks us to the skin.'

The rain held off until the fork in the road where Emily turned off for her parent's house in the group of houses, the smithy, church and vicarage that comprised the hamlet of

Broomfield. As the two girls said goodbye, large drops splashed onto their faces and Emily pulled off her shawl to further protect the tiny birds in her basket.

Amy did not wait to wave but set off towards home as the rain grew in force until she could feel each stabbing raindrop on her face and arms and its cold wetness penetrating her clothes. It became dark earlier than usual because the gathering rain clouds obliterated the last remaining rays of the sunset. Head down, Amy pressed on as the wind rose, tearing her wet hair and lashing it against her face. The puddles joined together to leave little or no dry place to tread and the track's edge grew less and less clearly defined. Amy was no stranger to harsh weather but this was extraordinary in its ferocity and she could only place one foot before the other towards her goal. Her eyes were barely able to penetrate the rain coming down now in sheets, aided by the wind. It was impossible to tell between the muddied track that squelched and yielded beneath her feet and the natural marsh that bordered the Blackwell land, and it was not until Amy almost fell over a tussock of marsh grass that alarm bells began to sound in her consciousness. She cast round for something to tell her the direction in which to turn but there was nothing to help; no tree or stone wall or hedgerow to mark her whereabouts. A dreadful panic came over her as she stood with water streaming down her face peering into the darkness. She felt her father drawing her in to the marsh where he lay cold and dead. She heard his laughter curling in the wind and she screamed at him to leave her alone. But she heard her voice lost in that same wind while his laughter grew louder as it swept towards her and an ice cold grip clutched at her throat.

Amy turned away from the sound and ran for her life, her skirts catching in briar and low bushes. It was not good judgement that led her back to the track and saw her staggering towards the lighted windows of the farm and into the outstretched arms of her mother who had opened the door for the umpteenth time to look out for her daughter. It was good fortune.

William sat, dominating the fire but got up irritably to close the door behind his sister while complaining of the draft.

'Make way for Amy to get near the fire, William. She is soaked to the skin.' Amy was sobbing and muttering about the marsh and the darkness but when her mother heard her father's name in the tumble of words, she wrapped the towel round Amy's head and rubbed her hair vigorously and muffled Amy's voice.

'It is time for your bed William. Besides, I have to get these wet clothes off your sister before she catches the ague.' William complained but did as he was told and mother waited until she heard the bedroom door close behind him.

'What ails you Amy? You have been in heavy rain before. Come pull off those wet things and wrap this blanket round you. Here, take this mug and drink it down.' Amy took the beaker, drank the orange liquid and gasped and coughed as its warm harshness caught her throat, followed by a warm glow that spread throughout her body.

'He was there mother,' Amy whispered, 'calling out to me and laughing as I trod towards him and the marsh. He was pulling me towards him so that he could drag me down with him. He is not dead, mother, is he? He is lying in wait to pull me down to him. Where can I go to get away?' Amy leapt up from the chair and circled the room naked but with the blanket trailing behind her. Her eyes were wild and seemed to search the room for a way out. Her hair was a tangled mess framing her white face. Alice Blackwell struck that face with the flat of her hand and caught the stunned girl in her arms as she collapsed into them.

*

Amy awoke to the familiar sounds of the farm. The sun shone through the kitchen window and its warm rays landed on the chair in which she had slept by the fire all night. She peered out from the shawl that wrapped her head, at her mother who was sleeping awkwardly in the other stick back chair by the window. Through the window, Amy could see steam rising from the fields that stretched up the hill topped by a little copse of trees. The events of the night before seemed very far away in the cheering morning sunshine. Later, as she fed the chooks who gathered urgently round her feet to peck up the dropped golden grain, she wondered if she might have imagined the rain and the wind and the voice. But the smell of the marsh was still in her nostrils and her clothes lay stretched out to dry on the hedges over by the door, testimony to her ordeal and reinforcing the events from which she would never escape.

7

The wedding was a simple affair with but three or four neighbours and their families in attendance. Amy wore a dress paid for by Charlie and worn with little appreciation by his cheerless bride. The wedding breakfast was held at the farm and provided with the help of the same good natured neighbours. William gave away his sister with a sour look on his face and disappeared during the wedding breakfast staying absent until late that night.

Amy's mother was forced to remind her daughter that the occasion was meant to be a happy one and to behave accordingly in front of the guests. When the time came for the happy couple to repair to their bedroom, they did so to cheers together with ribald remarks and winks from the menfolk. The flushed cheeks of the couple were considered normal and with relief they closed the door behind them.

With some difficulty, Amy managed to undress under cover of her voluminous nightdress and get into bed while Charlie stood helplessly by. His position became only too clear to him when Amy threw down one of her pillows and a blanket on the floor and blew out the candle.

Next morning, Charlie was down first and cleaned out and lit the fire before washing at the pump in the yard. When he came in with wet hair and streaming cheeks, mother was there waiting with a towel.

'It was good of you to light the fire, Charlie. I appreciate it.'

'T'was no trouble Mrs Blackwell. I am pleased to help.'

'Charlie...' began Mrs Blackwell. 'I peeped into the bedroom this morning and I saw... the arrangement Amy has for you.' Charlie coloured up. 'Many men would have expected more from their bride on their wedding night.' Charlie put up his hand to pass off the situation.

'No, Charlie. It was good of you. I appreciate that too. I ask that you be patient with her for I am sure that she will come round in the end. She has suffered much in her short life but once she sees that you are a kindly man and are of a gentle disposition, she will be more trusting, you'll see.'

Before Charlie could speak, William appeared at the foot of the stairs.

'Good morning William,' said Charlie amiably. William stared at him for a moment and then without reply pulled out a chair at the table.

'How long will breakfast be? There's work to be done.'

'William, a civil tongue would not come amiss,' said mother without turning from her stirring of the porridge.

'William, what would you have me do first?' asked Charlie.

'I thought it would be you telling me,' retorted William with a snarl.

'Tis your farm, William. I am here to help.' William grunted and set to with his porridge. When they had both finished, they got up and put on their coats at the door.

William said, 'We'll be back at midday.' Mother watched them as they crossed the yard. William had shot up recently and was only a head short of Charlie but broader in the shoulder like his father. He was just turned thirteen but already filling out into manhood. The life was hard and childhood was but a short season in the span of life in these times. She watched as they disappeared into the barn to tack up old Dexter and prayed fervently that this man would be kind to Amy and that their lives would not repeat the misery of her own. And then the thought of the new life that was in her daughter came to her and she smiled at the prospect. A baby would be a delight and no mistake. Her daughter was strong with broad hips and there was no reason to fear that she would have trouble with the birthing. The babe would surely bring about a bond between the two young folk. The thoughts gave her spirit and she hummed a little tune as she went about her chores.

8

The days and weeks went by and it was decided that William and the neighbours must be told about the impending birth of Amy's babe before she began to show. William appeared to be disinterested in the news and remained in an almost permanent bad mood. Amy displayed little pleasure in the prospect of her baby and only her mother and Charlie looked forward with pleasurable anticipation to the birth. Fortunately, due to Amy's youth and hard work, her body remained tight until well into the fifth month. And even then, her clothes concealed the slight mound of her belly for a month more. Each evening, as the winter nights drew in, mother would sit knitting or sewing tiny garments showing each to Amy when it was completed. Amy would glance over them to please her mother but she took no pleasure in them herself. The baby was not wanted by her. How different it could have been. Perhaps the corn-haired boy from the market would have courted her. They would have held hands like other couples she had seen. Perhaps they would have lain in the cornfields with their arms around each other while he kissed her lips. They might have married on a spring day, she with flowers in her hair, and the baby boy they would have made would have corn coloured hair like his father. She would have lived at his home, wherever that would be, away from this hated farm where she had always lived her life and they would have grown together with five babies more.

She felt that her father had stolen her life from her. Why should she want his ill-begotten brat? She did not understand the obvious joy her mother felt for this unborn creature.

As Amy's body became distended she felt more intensely the bitterness against the life she had been dealt. Her mother had put a mattress down beside her bed for Charles, though he had never complained. Alice Blackwell hoped with all her heart that the marriage would be consummated after the child had come and that Amy would see the good in Charlie, for he was a good man, hard working and thoughtful, if a little weak of character.

February came and went and March arrived with blustery winds and flurries of late snow that didn't settle but melted into the already sodden ground, making work on the farm muddy and difficult. It was good that the baby was due at this time for Amy had been able to stay in the house recently, the men well able to cope with the work at this time of year.

Amy's waters broke as she was about to serve supper on a Sunday evening. She stood in amazement, staring down at the puddle that spread dark on the quarry-tiled floor and the menfolk stared with her, embarrassed at the sight.

'You two, to the barn or wherever. And don't come back until you're called,' said mother.

'I'm off to the inn. There's no call for me here,' said William and put on his coat and went. Charles hovered in the kitchen but made no attempt to go.

'Charlie,' said mother sharply as Amy's first contraction clawed its way across her stomach. He still was rooted to the spot, his face ashen.

'What is it, Charlie. Did you not hear me?'

'What if the same happens as before?' he said in a hushed voice as if to himself. Mother understood at last and in a more kindly voice said,

'Don't be fearful, Charlie. It will be all right. Go now and I will make very sure that all goes well and before you know it you will have a son or daughter in your arms.' She pushed him gently to the door, placing his hat on his head and his coat over his arm. At the last minute, he glanced back to see Amy gripping the edge of the table with white knuckles while unfamiliar deep sounds came from her throat.

*

He settled himself in the hay next to old Dexter's stall and pulled the worn tweed coat round him. It was bitter cold and the late snow slanted past the open barn doors and the moonlight lit the yard intermittently as the clouds scurried before it. The clump of trees to the east of the farm stood out black-veined against the moon-lit sky, bending away from the wind. He saw a candle in their bedroom, flickering in the draft from the window and imagined he heard Amy's voice above the wind. He had been through this drama before and to what end? To find himself alone once more with nothing but a funeral to look forward to. He thought about his first wife. He had not loved her but he had grown used to her company. Compared to Amy, she was a plain girl and not bright and clever like Amy but she was of a happier disposition and easy to get on with, even during her waiting time. He wondered if the child would, at last, make Amy happy. He knew it would make him happy for he yearned for something to love that would love him back. He wondered if Amy would let him into her bed to hold her in his arms at last, for his desire for her had heightened over the months. He had often stared down at her while she slept, had even gently touched her bare shoulder, wondering at his good fortune, if only…

Hours had passed and he became conscious of a voice entering his thoughts. It was his mother-in-law calling from the open kitchen door. Was her voice happy or sad? He couldn't be sure. He was reluctant even to find out. She called his name again and the wind carried her joy across the yard to him. He leapt from the hay and dashed across the yard towards the lighted kitchen.

'You have a beautiful baby daughter, Charlie – yours from now on.'

'How is Amy?' he asked breathlessly.

'She is tired, for it was a long, hard delivery but she is well enough and will recover with sleep. You may go up to them for a moment – just a moment, mind, and I'll have a hot drink for you when you come down to warm you.'

Charlie went up the stairs two at a time to the attic bedroom and quietly opened the door. Amy lay on her pillows, white-faced but calm. Charlie stooped to kiss her forehead and she only slightly turned her head away but not unkindly. The baby was in a basket beside the bed and Charlie looked into it to see the smallest of human beings with a fine cloud of red hair and tiny hands that waved in the air above the cream knitted blanket. Charlie gently tucked the blanket over the little arms and when he turned back to Amy she was sleeping soundly, her own red hair spread across the pillows.

In the kitchen, Charlie found mother soaking sheets in a tub. There were two mugs of hot ale steaming on the table. At last she sat down with him. She looked tired and drawn but joyful.

'Well, what do you think, Charlie?'

'I am fair overwhelmed, mother,' for he called her that now. 'She is the most beautiful child and so pink and healthy looking.'

'What will you call her?'

'Oh tis Amy's choice. I will be happy whatever she be called.'

'You must choose between you Charlie. Amy must not always have her own way with you. She will think better of you if you are firm but kindly. Now – we must agree what to tell the neighbours. We will say that the baby came early and we will keep it hid saying that it is sickly because of it, or they will guess when they see that it is full term and as healthy as you or me. In good time we will have a Christening. Perhaps when she is at three months old. What do you say?'

'You are right of course but what of William?'

'He has not seen the babe yet and he knows nothing of such things. We will tell him the same for I cannot guarantee his silence in any of this.' Charlie nodded and took a drink.

'Now Charlie. I don't want to take away your pleasure in fatherhood by these untruths. Once they are told, we have no need to lie again for we are honest folk and I want us to live honestly. Tomorrow morning, you can go to the parson and tell him the good news and the story we are telling the neighbours. You must tell him also our plan for the Christening – in three months mind.'

They sat in silence hugging their mugs in two hands for the warmth from them.

'It will be a May Sunday and if the weather is kind, we will take the table outside and spread it with baking to celebrate the birth of my baby grand-daughter.' And with that, mother kissed Charlie's cheek and said,

'Goodnight, Charlie,' and went to bed.

Charlie sat for a long time watching the embers flicker and die in the hearth. His heart was so full that he knew he would not sleep and he didn't want to disturb Amy and the baby. At last he had a family, a wife and a baby daughter, both as beautiful as any man could wish. He felt the blood rush through his veins with energy. He wanted to leap in the air and shout at the top of his voice. He wanted to work in the fields and make the farm flourish for this family. For two pins he would go out now in the darkness and start work.

The door latch lifted and William came in barging into a chair as he attempted unsuccessfully to hang up his coat. He giggled stupidly as he looked down at the fallen garment but left it there and sank into a chair at the table, looking with bleary eyes at Charlie.

'Well. Is the brat born yet?' he asked thickly.

'William. Are you drunk?'

'What of it? Tis no business of yours. You have no sway in this house.'

'I do not pretend to it, William but I am just thinking of your mother and what she has suffered with your father. You must not let her see you like this.' William threw out an arm dismissively but knocked over a mug which smashed loudly on the floor. He giggled again and put his finger to his mouth with a 'Shshsh.'

'Go to your bed, William and sleep this off. Here, I'll help you up the stairs and in the morning you can find out that you are an uncle with a baby niece.'

When he had seen William collapse onto his bed, he threw a blanket over him and went back to the kitchen, settling himself to sleep by the remnants of the fire. His elation over the baby far outweighed any fleeting concerns he had about William.

*

At three months, as planned, baby Daisy was Christened and presented to the neighbours. Amy and her mother were congratulated for the healthy baby they had raised after a 'premature' birth. All the complications of life at the farm appeared to have straightened themselves out to the relief of Amy's mother and the parson, who was not dissatisfied with his labours in the matter.

The child was a happy and contented baby and Charlie's pride and joy. She had a head of curly red hair, pretty blue almond eyes and rosebud lips. Amy performed her motherly duties while Charlie was at work but was only too glad to hand her over to him as soon as he came through the door. Her mother took great pleasure from the babe but left her to Amy as much as possible in the hope that they would bond at some point.

It was Charlie who roused himself from his mattress on the floor when the child cried at night while Amy hardly stirred in her bed.

'Amy,' said her mother one morning after Charlie and William had left for the fields, 'Charlie has been very patient with you all this time, but you have a duty to treat him like a husband. Do you not think he has spent enough time sleeping on the floor? He works hard and is a good father to Daisy. Surely he deserves a bed after his labours and a kind word now and then?'

Amy looked up at her mother with a truculent look on her face. 'I cannot help how I feel.'

'And Charlie cannot help that his first wife and child died and that Daisy is not his own and despite all his efforts to please that his second wife hardly has a kind word for him. Remember that without him, we could not have managed the farm and would be destitute. William treats him poorly and gives him all the hardest work to do and goes and spends the money at the inn while Charlie supports us all keeping nothing for himself. Just think for a moment, girl, what we would do if he decided that life was not good for him here and he left – or even that he came across a girl who would be loving towards him.'

'He would not leave Daisy for he loves her too much.'

'A man has needs, Amy, and Daisy is not his.'

Amy thought for a while. 'I will let him into my bed so that he can rest well for work but more I cannot do. He is like a strange man to me.'

Her mother smiled. 'That is a good thing Amy and I know how hard it is for you.'

Before Charlie and William returned, they went up and rolled the mattress away and made up the bed for two. After her mother had gone back down to the kitchen, Amy placed her pillow firmly down the centre of the bed. She stood for a while studying the arrangement with her hands on her hips, then, satisfied went down to help her mother with the supper.

Charlie did not remark on the change when bedtime came. He took off his clothes in the dark and climbed carefully into the bed turning with his back to Amy and lying as still as he could. He lay for a long while staring into the darkness and then said, 'Thank you Amy. Goodnight.' She did not reply but he knew that she was awake and had heard him.

*

It was late July and the weather was humid and heavy. It had been a relief for Charlie to place his head under the pump in the yard and douse himself with the cold water when he came back from the fields. He drank thirstily, for the dust lined his throat and lungs and his eyes were sore from it.

'There's a storm brewing,' he said as he came into the kitchen.

'Twill clear the air,' said mother.

'Twill flatten our good corn too and we can do without that.'

Amy glanced up at the sky through the open door. 'I hate storms,' she said with wide eyes.

At about midnight, there was a loud thunder clap followed by a lightning flash. Soon after, there was another with but two or three seconds between. Amy tossed and turned in the bed.

'Tis coming this way,' warned Charlie, lying still. Just then, the thunder was overhead and shook the house with its explosion. Amy and Charlie both sat up and the lightning lit up the attic as it cracked above the roof.

'Charlie!' Amy screamed.

'Tis just a summer storm,' said Charlie soothingly and the thunder clapped again.

'Charlie, make it stop!' said Amy, flinging her arms round his neck.

Charlie froze, uncertain what to do. He placed one arm round the quivering body and as she clung harder, held her tightly making soothing sounds into her hair. They remained clinging to one another until the thunder had moved away.

'Are you all right now my dear?' said Charlie and let her go for fear that she would spurn him now.

'Yes Charlie. Thank you,' she said in a small voice.

'Will you sleep now?'

'I think so Charlie.'

When Charlie went up to bed the following night, he found that the pillow had been removed. His happiness was great but he was aware that the situation was a delicate one that could be spoiled with too amorous an approach. He longed to take Amy in his arms finally but her emotions were so fragile that he was fearful of her. They lay side by side with only a sheet over them for the nights were still hot and humid despite the storm. Charlie stared into the darkness aware of her body next to his, listening to her breathing. At last, it became regular and deep and her head fell onto his shoulder and then her arm was across his chest. He could not help smiling into the darkness with the pleasure of it and fell asleep himself with the lightest of hearts.

At breakfast, he noticed that Amy was humming a little tune to herself as she went about her chores and as he left for work she pressed a piece of bread and cheese and an apple wrapped in a kerchief into his hand and one for William.

'Thank you Amy. That will go down nicely at midday.' And they smiled at each other. Mother watched as Charlie and William crossed the yard, Charlie whistling as he walked. Then she looked at Amy whose cheeks were pink and whose eyes were bright and she sighed with satisfaction. If only she could rein in William from the way he was taking, her joy would be complete.

*

Charlie's patience was rewarded but not until another winter had passed. There was a full moon and its gentle light filled the attic with soft shadows. Charlie lay on his back with his hands behind his head and Amy suddenly climbed out of bed and stood in a pool of light. She undid the ribbon at her neck and allowed her nightdress to fall at her feet then unbraided her hair and shook it loose about her bare shoulders. Charlie surveyed with tearful eyes, the soft curves of her body then opened his arms as she climbed back into the bed beside him.

9

William was now seventeen. He had not put on any height but had thickened out with strong, broad shoulders and heavy thighs below slim hips. He frequented the public house on most nights and had a circle of friends from surrounding villages who were not the best of characters. He had learned to hold his drink in the main but they were a rowdy bunch and not popular with the locals.

'Like father, like son,' was the general opinion. On more than one occasion, he had got himself into a fight over some trivial occurrence and had had to be separated by some of the older men there. However badly hurt he was though, he always turned up for his work, even after a night's absence from home, for he was afraid that his hold on the farm would be in jeopardy if he did not. He had a strong feeling of ownership and no nice-as-pie infiltrator was about to steal it from under his nose.

Thomas was gone from the scene, was probably dead, and his father too, and he would marry. His sister and her offspring and husband could go and find their own place. He had nothing against Amy but she had chosen her lot and could live with it under some other roof.

Had he been pressed, he would have had to admit that Charlie was a good worker and that the farm would have gone under had he not been there to help. Still, if Charlie wanted to work his fingers to the bone for a farm that would never be his, that was his business. William was quite prepared to bide his time. With luck, by the time he was twenty one and could lay claim to the farm, it would be bringing in a fair return and he would be able to afford a labourer. As to his mother, she could go with Amy, for he did not want her accusing eyes on him every minute. He knew that she had grown fond of Charlie and that she did not approve of his own drinking habits.

Daisy, in the way of all small children, accepted William with all his faults and went to him, arms outstretched, when he came in at night and took his rebuff without question. Amy had now become a true mother to her, for her amiable character and prettiness were impossible to resist. Amy was now three months pregnant with Charlie's child and hoped fervently for a son. Charlie, on the other hand, was so filled with delight at his good fortune, that if Amy had produced half a dozen more daughters, he would be delighted, if they were all as pretty as his Daisy.

One night in November when the rain slashed against the window pains and the candles guttered with the draft from the cracks in them, all except William were seated round the table eating their evening meal while a good fire crackled in the grate. Daisy was dressed for bed and wrapped in a shawl while she drank her milk on granny's knee. Amy was now heavy with child and got up from her chair with difficulty to clear the plates. The latch lifted and Thomas walked in.

*

For some time everyone stared at him, stock-still where they stood or sat. He was so changed. He had a patch over one eye and one arm made a bulge inside his overcoat while the empty sleeve hung free. If Thomas was changed, so too was the scene he saw before him; his sister grown into a woman in the last stages of pregnancy, a strange man at the table as if he was part of the family and a small child the image of Amy when she was his little toddling sister. There was no sign of his father and for this he felt relief. Nor any sign of his little brother William in the group. At last, mother dashed to him and embraced him.

'Tom, you're home safe and sound. We had given up hope,' and she put her head on his wet shoulder and wept into it. Amy rushed to him too and he put his one good arm round their shoulders as best he could. Charlie rose but held back.

'And who have we here?' asked Tom.

Amy drew back and pulled Charlie forward by the hand. 'This is my husband Charlie and this little treasure is our daughter Daisy. Sit down Tom, sit down and take off that wet coat.'

Tom unbuttoned the coat with his good hand and slid it from his shoulders displaying a heavily bandaged stump strapped to his chest.

'Oh Thomas,' said his mother. 'What has become of you?' The tears welled up in her eyes as she looked at her maimed son.

They sat for long hours as Thomas told of his exploits in the war and how he had outlived many of his friends and comrades. Daisy fell asleep on his lap and was put to bed, hardly stirring as her father carried her up the stairs.

Thomas told how he had lost one eye when a bullet had ricocheted off a nearby building and when he recovered he had insisted on returning to the front. But now, he had lost his left forearm in hand to hand fighting and was of no further use to the army and here he was, of little use to man nor beast. Amy went and put her arm round him.

'We are so pleased to have you back Tom... We have the man and that is all that matters.'

'And where is my father and William?' Tom asked. Amy quickly glanced at her mother.

'Your father said he was going after you to fetch you back and we have not seen hide nor hair of him since. The parson fears him dead for you know how he drank and got into fights,' said mother. 'William is probably at the inn where he spends much of his time when he is not working,' she added sadly.

'So my little brother has decided to follow in his father's footsteps.'

'He is not violent, Tom. Not in the same way.' she said hastily.

'I hope not with all my heart.'

'But you look so tired and I can see that your wound is hurting you. I will make a bed in William's room and you can rest.' And with that, she went up the stairs to do it.

'So Charles. You have been working the farm with William. From what I could see in the darkness, the fields are in good order and well up to season.' Charles spoke for the first time.

'I have done my best. The land is good round here and with proper husbandry shows good yield. I hope it meets with your approval.'

'I'm sure it will and I thank you for it and the way you have looked after my family. They look well on it. But I'm sorry, I must go to my bed for I can barely keep my one eye open,' he smiled.

*

Amy and her mother waited up for William so that he would not come upon Tom in his room and be shocked. When he eventually clattered through the door, he was in a bad way and had clearly been fighting.

'What's this?' he cried when he saw his mother and Amy sitting beside the dying embers of the fire. 'Am I to have a welcoming committee when I come home?'

'Look at the state of you William. Let me bathe those cuts.'

'Leave me be,' he shouted. 'You should see the other man,' and he laughed without amusement. He waved his mother away. 'Why are you not in your beds?'

'It is Tom. He has come home from the wars. He is sleeping in your room at this moment.'

William looked at them through hazy eyes, his head moving from side to side unsteadily as he tried to focus.

'Tom?' he said with little comprehension of what they had said.

'Oh, pull yourself together you drunken sot,' cried Amy with frustration. 'Can you not understand a simple statement?'

Mother put up her hand to stop any further discourse for their raised voices would awaken the household.

'Thomas is home for good and you can speak to him in the morning but for now, go and sleep off the state you are in and be quiet as you go up the stairs.'

William made no attempt to move but just stared at them trying to take in the news and what it might mean to his future plans. Amy took hold of one arm and mother the other and together they marched him up the stairs and he fell face down on to his bed. They threw a blanket over him and pulled off his boots and as Thomas stirred in his sleep, William joined him and their snores vibrated the bed posts and reverberated along the floor boards on which they stood.

Mother smiled to herself for she was sure that with Thomas' influence, she would get her youngest son back from the brink of wickedness and Tom, her beloved eldest son whom she had thought dead was home again. Here, under one roof was her entire family – everyone she loved – and no longer did they all have to live in fear and dread. She bent and stroked Tom's forehead then left for her own bed.

10

Tom's wounded arm made good healing progress but his frustration at being unable to work the farm machinery or even to tack up old Dexter, who was growing crochety in his old age, grew daily. He would slam into the kitchen at mid-morning, pull out a chair and sit with his head in his one good hand then pounding his forehead with his fist, curse the soldier who had slashed off his arm.

'I am fit for nothing, mother,' he would say, near to tears.

'There is no need for you to work for Charlie and William can manage.'

'And what do you suggest I do with my worthless life? Sit by the fire and smoke a pipe watching you work at your age and Amy, in her condition?' Mother stroked his forehead.

'The Lord gave you two eyes so that when one is put out, the other can take over – just as yours has done. He gave you two arms for the same reason and you will find ways of working with one good strong arm. Why, I knew a farmer once who lost a leg to a bull. He managed until the day he died with a wooden leg he carved for himself. They say that he wore down three wooden legs before that day came.' Tom looked up and smiled at his mother.

'You have an answer for all things, mother but I've a mind to tie one of your hands behind your back for a day and see how you manage the washing and the baking.' and with that he laughed and got up, grabbed a fresh-baked biscuit cooling on the rack and closed the kitchen door behind him.

When Amy's waters broke this time, Charlie had company in the barn. He and Tom sat side by side in the hay with a flagon of ale.

'You've a fine family Charlie and no mistake,' said Tom.

'And so you will have one day.'

'And who will want me with but one eye and one hand. I cannot feed myself, never mind a wife and family. If it were not for you Charlie...' and Tom buried his head in the other man's shoulder.

'Thomas, you must not think in this way. You have fought for your country and should be proud while I, I have just taken on an already well established farm and sat warm and cosy in your parlour. You will find a place in this world that will suit you, mark my words. Listen! Is that mother calling?'

'No. It's but the wind. Take another draught.'

'No. I must stay sensible in case I'm needed.'

Amy was safely delivered of a son, his head covered in a down of dark hair like his father's. They called him little Tom after his uncle and Thomas was touched by the honour they had done him. Thomas' arm had healed well and he was beginning to cope with the day to day tasks of the farm despite his disability. He could tack up old Dexter using his teeth to aid his one hand. And he could even plough a reasonably straight furrow to relieve the others while they took a break. He was growing stronger by the day in both mind and body. Life on the farm was good save for William's bouts of drunkenness and his mean disposition. Thomas tried to talk to him but he bade him mind his own business and continued in his behaviour.

William had been mightily put out by Thomas' return and by Charlie's growing entrenchment in the life of the farm. He saw his prospects falling away from him and the plan for him to take over the farm on his twenty first birthday fade into oblivion. What if he were to marry? There was no room for all of them here and he didn't see why he should be the one to leave. Thomas had abandoned them to their fate and had been welcomed home like a prodigal son and Charlie was an outsider. He was the only one who had been a constant worker of the farm yet his mother never recognised this in her adoration of the others. What if he did have a drink now and then. Surely he deserved some leisure time to himself? There was little enough pleasure to be had out of this life. He began to formulate a new plan for the future. He was but nineteen and there was plenty of time and still work to be done about the farm to make it worth more. He would spend the next two years encouraging the expansion of the flock; perhaps take on more cattle; even clear some more woodland for an extra field.

*

A year passed and then almost another when even William could not have planned for the opportunity that presented itself. The winter had been unusually dry and spring brought little in the way of rain to moisten the parched ground. All the surrounding farmland suffered from the drought and the newly planted crops were decimated. Those farmers who had not been frugal were in dire straits. One morning, men's voices were heard outside as the family were seated having breakfast before the day's work began. Then loud knocking on the door.

'Thomas, Charlie, William. Come with us quickly,' the men called out.

The three men got up and went out to find out what was amiss.

'Keep the women there and come with us,' they said.

'What is it?' asked Thomas pulling on his coat.

'The sheep strayed on to the marsh looking for fodder. We went to fetch them back for you and we found something in the dried out marshland,' said one man pushing to the front.

Thomas, Charlie and William followed the men down the track and along by the pasture towards the flatland and the marsh. The ground was cracked for lack of water and hard as nails.

'This way,' cried the men, beckoning the others to follow them.

'Watch your footing for it may look firm,' said another. At last they stopped and one of them pointed ahead. The rotting and decayed shape of a hand and arm stuck out of the mire that was cracked and crumbling like day old porridge in a saucepan. It took the rest of the day for the men to prise the body from its festering grave with hooks and spades and ropes. Despite its degeneration, it was clearly the body of Fred Blackwell

11

The magistrate and parson deliberated for some time and came to the conclusion that Fred Blackwell had got himself into a fight with some vagabond or other and fallen into the bog on his way home in a drunken stupor. Death by misadventure was the conclusion and a proper grave was dug for him in a corner of the churchyard with a modest wooden cross.

Amy and her mother suffered some sleepless nights during this time but when the matter was over, the family returned to its usual routine. All, that is except for William.

William had thought long and hard about his father's body in the bog. He remembered well the sight of him in the ashes in the kitchen and the state of Amy and his mother; the tale they had told him of his father's recovery from his so-called unconsciousness and his departure to follow Tom and fetch him back. He already knew about Amy's baby for he had heard the conversation between the parson and his mother on the night that Charlie had been brought to the farm to be her future husband. He had kept the knowledge to himself, sure that it would come in useful at some point. But now, now he had all the ammunition he needed, much more indeed than he had ever dreamed of.

He took his time for there was a pleasure in the contemplation of how he would use the knowledge to his own ends. He imagined their faces when he confronted them with it; how they would tremble and beg. The parson was helpless because of his complicity in their lies and even the magistrate had turned a blind eye to some of it.

William became swaggering and arrogant in his disposition. He would wander about the farm refusing to do the work that was needed, leaving it to Tom and Charlie. He spent even more time at the inn and boasted to his friends that he was soon to come into some property. They pushed him for more information saying that they didn't believe him but he was resolute in his statements and would not be pressed. He savoured every moment, even putting off his plan the more to enjoy the prospect.

One night, he staggered home earlier than usual to find the family seated round the kitchen fire. He shoved open the door and banged it closed after him, leaning against it for support.

'Well, this is a pretty sight and no mistake. The Blackwell family all together, sitting round the fire of an evening. It fare pulls at my heart strings, so it does.'

'Sit down William for you are drunk again, and keep your voice down for you will wake the babes,' said Tom, getting up to help him.

'Take your hands from me, Thomas. I've no need of your help. I know what I'm doing.' spat William at him. 'Yes, all of you here at the fireside… except my father.'

'William. You know that your father is dead.' said his mother softly. 'Surely you are not too drunk to remember that?'

'Aye, he's dead all right, just as he was in the hearth that you sit round so cosy now.'

Mother's face went pale and she dropped the knitting she was holding onto the floor.

'What ails you William? What are you gibbering about?' asked Tom.

'Why don't you ask your adoring mother and Amy here? There are more secrets under this roof than there are tiles upon it to keep out the weather.'

'Mother. Do you know what he is talking about?' said Tom. William did not let her speak.

'Aye mother, tell him how you killed our father and put him in the bog to rot.'

Mother buried her head in her hands and a faint wailing sound came from her.

'Mother?' said Tom.

'And Amy. Tell how you got yourself in trouble with some lad or other and the parson had to find you a husband double quick so that you would not give birth to a bastard child. And Charlie, who could not find a bride for himself and let himself pretend and the neighbours think that he'd courted Amy and that Daisy was his own.' William was now in full flood and his words tumbled from his drunken mouth in a cascade of barely audible words. 'And Charlie, tell Tom how you slept on the floorboards for months after you were married for you had not the backbone to demand your rights as a husband. I would not be surprised if little Tom is not some other man's child.'

'That is enough William. You are drunk and don't know what you're saying. T'were it not for that, I would lay you out upon this very floor.' Charlie was up on his feet and his face was red with anger.

'Sit down Charlie,' ordered Thomas. 'William, you will be quiet now for I want to understand from my mother from where these accusations come. These are dangerous words you speak William and I hope for all our sakes that it is the drink that has sparked your imagination. Now mother, if you are recovered enough?'

'Thomas, my dear son, I fear that there is some truth in what he says but he is not accurate and I must tell you how all these terrible things came about.'

'Tis about time and… ' started William.

'You will be quiet William, or I will fell you myself with my one good arm.'

'It was soon after you had left to enlist, Thomas,' began his mother. 'Your father came home drunk that night and sent us all to bed. All except Amy.' Tears began to stream down her cheeks as she talked. 'You know how it was Tom. Amy is a good girl.'

'I know, I know mother and I cannot forgive myself for not trying to stop him and for leaving like a coward.' Tom touched his head with his hand and closed his eye as though his head hurt at the thought.

'This time of which I speak, Amy resisted him, fought him off unable to take any more. The bread knife lay upon the table from supper and she caught it up and plunged it in his chest. It was in defence Tom — to defend herself.' She paused for breath and Tom went and sat beside her, his good arm about her shoulders.

'She was horrified at what she had done and called me down. We sent William away to his bed and together, we took the body, wrapped in a blanket, to the marsh where it was sucked up, we thought forever. Tom, I could not see Amy suffer any more for the sins of her father. We told everyone that he had gone after you to fetch you back. But it was not to end there for his wickedness remained after him. Amy found that she was with child by him.' Tom could not help an intake of breath.

'We went to the parson for help. We told him who had fathered the child and he promised to help us. Charlie here was the good man he found to husband Amy and take on Daisy as his own. Charlie has been kindness itself and loved Daisy as his own for he had lost a wife and child in childbirth before. He has been a good and thoughtful husband to Amy and I believe they love each other now. Little Tom is truly the son they have between them. Without this man,' and mother looked towards Charlie as she spoke, 'this farm would have been laid to waste and I would not have had the joy of my grandchildren in my old age.' Mother took a deep breath and rested her head on Tom's shoulder, exhausted by her long narrative.

'Believe that if you like but it makes no difference. My father was murdered and Daisy is a bastard child. Nothing can change that,' said William, fighting hard against the sleep that was trying to take him over.

'I wish you had told me before, mother. I could have shared your burden,' said Tom sadly. 'You did what you had to do to keep the family together and you'll get no blame from me. It is partly my fault that I did not stay to protect you. Had I done so, none of this might have happened.'

At last Amy spoke. 'Our mother has been a tower of strength in all this, Tom, and no one is to blame except our father. There is good that has come out of it, for I would not have Charlie for my husband and our two beautiful children. As for you Tom, you would not have gone to the army and lost an arm and an eye had my father not driven you away. He was the wickedest of men Tom and I am glad he is dead.' Amy broke down in tears and ran to Charlie for comfort.

William roused himself again. 'Whatever you say, murder was done and you must suffer the consequences.'

'No one will suffer any more,' said Tom. 'It is all in the past and shall remain there.'

'Oh, I don't think so,' smiled William with a leer. 'For what if I tell the authorities what I know?'

'You will not do that William.' said Tom with a voice of authority.

'There is a way that I will keep my council.'

'What have you to say?'

'For my silence, you will all have to pay. I will have the farm and you will find yourselves a living elsewhere. For that I will keep quiet and you can live your lives in peace.'

'That is preposterous William. Where should we go?'

'That is your problem and as you are all so good at solving problems when they arise, it should not prove too difficult for you. And now I must go to my bed and am not to be woken in the morning, for I have a mind to sleep in.' With that, William rose to his feet and lurched over to the stairs, mounted them and closed the bedroom door behind him.

Thomas sat with his mother far into the night having sent Amy and Charlie to bed.

'I fear that William is hell bent on this undertaking, mother.' said Thomas.

'What in heaven's name are we going to do? I always knew that he was his father's son but this wickedness is unexpected. Perhaps he will have forgotten it by the time that morning comes?'

'I fear not, mother. It is true that if he were to marry, the farm might not support us all nor the house shelter us all. I suppose I had not thought clearly of the future.'

'But the farm falls to you Tom as the eldest son. It should not be your concern.'

'You must look at it from William's point of view. I left the place and he has remained throughout. Charlie is not family except by marriage. It pains me though that he has thought to use his knowledge for blackmail. It would have been better had we all sat down to discuss the problem as a family together rather than be split asunder by the terrible happenings of the past. He knew what our father was like and that the events were not of our making. I hoped he loved us all enough to trust that we would never do wrong by him,' he finished sadly.

'He is too much like his father and I think that will never change.' replied mother.

'We can but appeal to his better nature tomorrow and hope that we can come to some arrangement,' said Tom getting up. 'We will go to our beds and pray that morning brings a happier time.'

12

Morning did come, all too soon. William stayed in his bed as promised and breakfast was taken by the rest in silence before departure for the fields. Only the children's happy voices broke the heavy spirit that lay upon the grown-ups. When William did appear, he was in jovial mood and demanded breakfast with some fried bacon for his bread. After he had eaten, mother sat down opposite him at the table.

'William,' she said. 'We are a family together. I love you, for you are my youngest child. We must hold together when troubles arise and not use them to divide us. You know that there is always a place for you here. That has never been in dispute. I can understand how you may be concerned that you will be pushed out but that would never happen. If you meet a girl and marry, we can build a house for you here on the land. What do you say?'

'That is all very well and good mother but I have a mind to have the whole farm to myself. If Tom had been killed in the war I would still have ousted Charlie and Amy and their screaming brats. I have plans for this place. If you stay, I will always be the youngest to be told what to do and expected to comply. If Charlie is such a golden boy, he can find a place of his own and take Tom with him for he is only half a man now and no use to me.'

'These are harsh words William and not worthy of you. And what of me? What would you do with me? Would you turn over your own mother to the magistrate? For it was I who buried your father in the bog and I who went to the parson for help and I who delivered your father's sin from your own sister.'

'You can go with Amy and Charlie for you dote on those brats of theirs.'

'So you would turn me out of my own house?'

'I will do what I have to to take what is my due. Now I have talked enough mother. Clear up this place for I will be back for my dinner before long.' He pushed away his plate, got up and, taking his coat from his father's hook by the door, went through it and closed it behind him.

Mother and Amy went about their morning chores in low spirits.

'I had hoped that all the bad things were behind us,' said Amy as she set the table for the mid-day meal.

'I suppose the happiness we have all had over the past few years was too much to ask,' replied her mother, her face grey with strain. I cannot take any more of this.' She sank down upon a chair and put her head in her hands. Amy went to her and put her arms round her.

'You must not let this thing bear down on you mother. Charlie and Thomas are here to help us now and they will think of something, never fear.' She was concerned at the look of her mother. She had never seen her so disordered. Her strength seemed to have ebbed from her and she looked suddenly old and quite frail. 'You must sit and rest and I will get you a little brandy to fortify you.' Her mother took the draught from her and sipped it slowly but the glass trembled so that she had to steady it with her other hand. Amy touched her mother's forehead and was troubled by the heat and sweat she felt upon it. 'I think you should go to your bed for a while, mother.' Mother pushed her hand away and got up to carry on with her work. 'I'm well enough, Amy.' But a dizziness came over her and she had to clutch the back of a chair to steady herself. The door opened and William came through it demanding his food.

'What ails you, mother?' he said glancing at her face and the way she stood trembling now from head to foot.

'She is not well, William. You have upset her with your threats. She is not a young woman any more and cannot suffer this agitation.'

'And what would you have me do? Twiddle my thumbs until she turns up her toes? That would suit you all very well, would it not?'

Amy glared at William but before she could remonstrate with him for his unkind words, he had scraped back his chair and flung out of the door.

Mother let out a little cry and crumpled to the floor quite gently as if her frame had softened and no longer supported her. Amy dashed to her just as Thomas and Charlie came in.

'What's this?' cried Thomas, helping Amy to lift their mother onto a chair. Charlie fetched a glass of water and held it to her lips but she did not drink.

'All this trouble has been too much for her and William has been here talking roughly to her,' said Amy, and then, 'Quiet children. Your granny is not well.' The children had rushed in from playing in the yard when they had seen their father and uncle come home.

'Come, my dear,' said Thomas lifting his mother with his one strong arm. 'It is bed for you for a few days and soon rest will bring you back to your old self once more.' He helped her up the stairs whispering soothing words as they went.

'I am sorely worried about her Charlie. I have never seen her in this state.'

'You must not concern yourself, Amy, my dear. All this is bound to have upset her but she has a strong constitution and will soon recover. It falls to us to find a way to relieve her concerns and we will, Amy. We will.' He pulled her to him and rested his face in her hair.

13

In her own way, mother gave the family one last gift – time. It was all she had to give for her failing health and her bedridden state precluded all else. Even William did not press the matters he had brought to bear on that terrible evening a few short weeks before. He was aware of the strength of feeling that would have risen against him had he but mentioned the farm and his intention to own it. He kept well away for most of the time, sloping in for his meals or up to his bed after the inn had closed for the night. Amy was heard to be constantly railing at the children for their noise, afraid that they would disturb her mother not realising that the sound of their voices was a comfort to her as she lay half in, half out of slumber.

The doctor, when finally called, could offer little in the way of hope for her recovery for he said that she seemed to lack the will for it. He could find no major cause for her illness but pointed out that she was a good age, particularly for a woman who had suffered a hard country life.

'I know he was your father, Thomas, but the one good thing that husband of hers did was to leave her with but three children to bear and raise for it is small in number for country folk round these parts. Remember that Charlie, if you value your wife. Restraint and consideration are everything in a marriage. Well, I must be upon my way. Make sure that your mother drinks plenty of fluids. Try and maintain her temperature by bathing her forehead with cold water and also try to get her to take a little broth each day.' He shrugged his shoulders as if to say that it was all he could recommend, placed his broad-brimmed hat upon his head and went out to his horse and trap waiting in the yard.

Alice Blackwell lingered in and out of consciousness for ten more days and Amy nursed her with full attention while Charlie took the children with him to work. On the tenth day, she opened her eyes and seemed fully conscious, calling for Amy. Amy propped her up on her pillows with rising hope that this was a sign of her recovery. Mother seemed to desire to talk to her and Amy wetted her lips with water from the glass at her side.

'Amy, I am going now. You will take my place and you will be strong. I know you will. Tell Thomas and Charlie and my dear children that you have all made my last years the happiest in my life.' She seemed exhausted but reached for Amy's hand and pressed a tiny gold cross on a chain into her palm and closed her fingers round it. 'I've worn this cross of my mother's under my bodice and now it is yours Amy my dearest daught… er.' Her head fell to one side and she was gone.

*

Amy was inconsolable over the following days and Thomas too took the death of his mother hard. Charlie was a rock on whom they could depend throughout the funeral and the days before and after it although he felt the loss almost as much as if she had been his own flesh and blood. Only William seemed unaffected but had the decency to work the farm while the others attended to the matters in hand. The neighbours remarked at his good nature in working through his sorrow to save the others and the family was not about to disillusion them. The good people were not, however, aware that he had already moved his things into her bedroom and occupied her bed before it was barely cold.

It rained heavily on the day of the funeral as it so often does. They all stood like black hooded crows around the gaping hole, hardly feeling the wetness soak into their clothes as the realisation that they would never see their mother and neighbour again struck home. Amy was taking it hard for she had spent every hour with her mother and learned to depend on her for each decision of the day; the food they prepared, the care of the domestic animals, the cleaning of the house. She had even delivered Amy's children. How could she bear to be without her? Even Charlie, the man she loved for a husband had come to her on the instigation of her mother. She turned to him now for solace and he put his arm about her, understanding her sorrow.

Thomas stood at the graveside and recalled much of his mother's wise advice and the guilt at leaving her to his father's harsh treatment fell heavily upon him. He asked for her forgiveness in a whisper as he dropped soil onto the coffin in the hole, the rain turning the earth to mud around it.

William stayed long enough to do what had to be done then left, skulking across the graveyard with his head hunched down into his shoulders and his hands in his pockets.

Charlie passed his sleeping boy to Amy and helped Daisy toss small clods of soil onto the coffin then took off his hat and stood, head bent in genuine reverence for the woman who had given him Amy and his children and a happy roof over his head in return for so little for herself.

The parson completed his words and those gathered turned to go, picking their way through the long grass to the path and then to the road that led to the farm. Amy hurried ahead, glad of something to occupy her for she expected quite a few neighbours would arrive wanting refreshment and a warm place to dry out. William's threats must be forgotten for the moment.

*

The days that followed were hardest for Amy for she was now alone in the house for much of the day. Soon, Daisy would start at the village school and Amy would lose even her constant chatter to keep her company. Little Tom was a quiet child, playing for hours at a time on his own. Charlie had carved him some wooden toys representing animals on the farm and old Dexter and his cart and he would sit outside in all weathers playing with them in the sand and gravel of the yard. Charlie came home at midday at first to see how she was coping and to give her company for an hour but soon, the work on the farm demanded that he gave his entire day to it.

Nothing was said about William's threats and it was hoped generally that he had put them aside. But one evening, he did not go to the inn but sat after his evening meal and smoked his pipe while Amy cleared the table.

'I have given you all time to consider my demands,' he announced all of a sudden. 'Nothing has changed in my mind and it should be easier for you now that you have not mother to consider.'

'William, surely you do not intend to persist with this notion of yours?' said Thomas.

'I have made it clear enough. Either you all go or Amy will have to face the magistrate for what she has done. In my mind it is fair. If I killed a man I would hang for it. I am giving her the chance to live in return for the farm and the living I have worked all my life.'

'Take the farm if you have a mind to, William. We will draw up deeds to say that it is yours but allow us to remain here where we were all born and we will run it as you would have it run. What do you say?' said Thomas.

William smiled as he watched their faces all turned to him for his decision. He sat puffing on his pipe as if deep in thought.

'I think... not,' he said at last.

'Then you would cast us out, even the children, with no roof over our heads?'

'I will give you three months during which time I shall expect you to work under my direction. After that time, it is up to you. The door will be locked against you and your possessions out in the yard.'

He rose and put on his coat and went now to the inn.

Thomas and Charlie sat together in the kitchen after sending a distraught Amy to bed.

'Thomas, I am not of this family save by marriage and I will do whatever you consider is best but I cannot, will not see Amy suffer after all she has been through. You know I would lay down my life for her.'

'I know, I know, Charlie. I too but I am only half a man and feel helpless in all this. Had I never gone away...'

'We cannot change the past, Tom. We must look to the future and whatever it brings. Your mother would have said as much.'

'Tomorrow is market day. I will go there and speak to the farmers and see if there is work to be had. It would be a start, would it not? Will you give me leave to offer you as a whole man, Charlie, for it is unlikely that they would consider me?'

14

Tom slipped out of the house at dawn and walked the eight miles to the market town of Barton Underwood. The place was crowded and noisy with the cries of animals and men; stall holders set out their wares and horses drew carts full of vegetables and fruit for sale. Tom pushed through the crowd and bought a pie for his breakfast from the boy with the tray of pies balanced on his head, the warm aroma of fresh baking wafting down from it. Then on down the cobbled street strewn with limp, cast off vegetables and straw in the mud and into the main ring where beasts with steam rising from their flanks milled together. He sought out some farmers of his acquaintance. The kindly men asked after his family having heard of their loss.

'I'm looking for work,' he told them after assuring them of the family's good health, 'for my brother-in-law and myself'. They looked at him amazed. 'But,' said one, 'you have a good living in that farm. Why should you want extra work?' Tom was reluctant but was forced to tell them that William had claimed the farm on his twenty first birthday and wanted all of them gone by three months hence. They were astonished at his news but the long and short of it was that they could not offer him any help in the matter. He went from one group to another and was met with the same incredulity and the same negative response.

Nearing the end of the day, Thomas was preparing to return to the farm when he was nearly run down by a handcart full of plants and young saplings pushed by the head gardener from the Hall.

'Look lively there,' said the man in a jovial voice. 'Is it not Thomas Blackwell I near flattened with my cart? You look as though you could do with a pint of ale, for that is where I am heading – to the inn to quench my thirst.'

'I will come with you Frank Turner, and gladly,' said Tom.

They walked together to the inn off the square and Frank Turner parked his cart under the window where he would be able to keep an eye on it from within. Soon they sat with two tankards of frothing ale before them and the welcome warmth from a large log fire burning in the iron grate in the open fireplace at the end of the room. The high, beamed ceiling was barely visible for the smoke cast by the fire and the smoking of many pipes, but the atmosphere was otherwise jovial and men drank in celebration of the satisfactory deals made with one another, or because they wished to drown their sorrows.

'You seem much pre-occupied since last I saw you Tom, for you appeared to have overcome your war wounds and settled into life in the old country surrounded by your family. Of course you lost your father long since but if you will pardon my forthrightness, he was not an asset to the family from what I heard?'

'Aye, you heard right, Frank and I'll speak of him no more for he is best erased from our memories.'

They nodded to each other in agreement and took a draught of beer.

'You heard that my mother passed away recently?'

'No I did not Thomas and I'm right sorry to hear it. She was a good woman, respected by all in the district. You were as favourably blessed with her, Thomas as you were disadvantaged by... er, he that we are not about to mention.' said Frank awkwardly. 'That is the reason for your long face then Tom?'

'No, for although I miss our mother I know that she was happy at the end. It is another business that occupies me. It is our William. He has turned one and twenty and desires to take over the farm and turn us all onto the street.'

'What? But has he the right?'

'He says that I left the farm and that Charlie Marriot, my brother-in-law is only there by marriage. He says also that I am but half a man and of no use to him. There is some truth in what he says, Frank but it is hard and he means to stick with it, giving us three months to vacate.'

'This is bad news indeed, Tom and I'm sorry for it.' He sat in silence for a bit, supping his ale thoughtfully.

'There is soon to be work up at the Hall but it is heavy labouring and there will be only quarters for the men while they are there. The new mistress is bent on creating an I-talian sunken garden with a bridge and water gardens alongside. Tis beyond me even though I've studied the plans til my head aches but there be work there for many months, even years it seems to me.'

'Well it sounds as though it is work that Charlie at least could put his hand to, and it is the only work I've heard of in the whole day here.'

'I reckon that the pay will be good enough and Charlie would be able to support his wife and bairns at least. Though, as to a roof over your heads, I cannot help you there.'

Thomas downed the remainder of his ale and scraped back the bench as he stood to go.

'You have been a tower of strength to me Frank Turner and I thank you for it.' He held out his hand.

'Wait!' said Frank. 'I can do more. I shall need extra hands in the garden when planting comes and one strong hand on a man with sense in his head is worth two, or four on men with none. You could board with me and my wife for we have an estate cottage with two bedrooms and no children to fill them. Sadly, we could not house your sister and her family as well.'

'You are a man with the biggest heart, Frank and I thank my stars for bumping into your cart this noon time. I cannot thank you enough and would be glad to take up your offer on both counts.' They shook hands warmly and Thomas pushed his cap to the back of his head and whistled his way through town and was still to be heard whistling on the long road back to the farm.

Thomas had determined not to tell William of the events of the day for there was still much to be settled; the problem of Amy's lodging and the children for one. He waited until William had departed for the inn that evening after complaining of Thomas' absence from work that day. Thomas said nothing by way of explanation but took William's grievance without comment.

'You should not let him talk to you like that,' said Amy. 'He has not the right.'

'It is of no consequence, Amy. Besides, I have things to tell you. Leave that now and come and sit down. I have managed to overcome some of our problems if it behoves you, Charlie, to take up the work on offer.' He told them of the work soon to be available at the Hall and Charlie agreed that he would do whatever it took to support Amy and the children despite Thomas' warning that it would be heavy work such as a navvy would undertake, also that it would demand that he lived on site in the quarters provided. He also told them of the gardening that he, Thomas, had been offered and the lodging that went with it.

'All that remains is for us to find suitable lodging for Amy and the children,' he finished.

'You have done remarkably well for us,' said Charlie. Amy was not so gratified.

'We shall all be separate. I cannot bear the thought. I hate William for treating us so.' The tears ran down her face and Charlie went to comfort her.

'Perhaps it will be only for a while, Amy my dear. Who knows, Thomas and I may make enough money to find a small place for us all.' But Amy was not to be consoled.

'We have time yet before we must vacate to find something close at hand for you and the children, Amy, and already Charlie and I are on the same estate and will see something of each other in the day. It is hard, I know but something tells me that William will not find the running of the farm quite as easy as he supposes. He may be glad to come cap in hand and ask for our return before long. He has not been accustomed to make decisions or to put back money into the stock and seed. He has always considered his money for pleasure and there will be little time for that. He has not thought who will cook and clean either. He will have to pay for that service too.'

'Of course, you are right Tom. I had not thought about that. Nor do I think he has.' Amy was buoyed up by Thomas' remarks.

'Charlie and I will put our heads together and find a roof for you and the children, never fear.'

*

The days passed and work on the farm was overseen by William with scant regard for the fairness of the load and with little assistance from himself. Nothing had been said of the work that had now been confirmed at the Hall and William in his ignorance looked forward with cruel pleasure to the day when he could lock out his family and cast their belongings into the yard.

Thomas meanwhile, asked about for lodgings for Amy and the children but with no success. After a sleepless night, he rose very early and left before the others were awake, walking once more the road to town. But this time, he veered off the road where the gates to the Hall stood closed still for the night. He sat against a tree near the gates until the gatehouse door opened and the keeper emerged rubbing the sleep out of his eyes. Thomas rose and came to the gates, doffing his cap with a good morning for the gate keeper.

'I have business up at the Hall kitchens,' he said.

'Is it you Thomas Blackwell? Why did you not make yourself known? I would not have challenged you,' he smiled. 'My eyes grow dim with age. They say that I am short-sighted for I can read a page of writing but the distance is a blur to me. But what happens over the hill is of no business of mine so I have no need to see it, say I,' and he laughed his amiable laugh. 'What brings you here, Tom?'

'I look for work for my sister Amy. She is a good girl and a hard worker but too shy to come herself.'

'I would think that she had enough to occupy her with two bairns and the likes of you menfolk to look after. The farm makes a good living or so I hear.'

'Aye, it does but my brother William lays claim to it for himself and wants us out in but two months time. Charlie, her husband will work on the new building work and I on the gardening. We are fortunate in finding work so quickly.'

'I am amazed at your news Tom. I had heard that your brother was the son of his father in more ways than one and I have seen him with my own eyes on more than one occasion causing trouble at the inn and outside it but, this is cruel indeed.' He rubbed his chin with his fist and shook his head from side to side. 'I wish you luck Thomas,' he said waving as Tom started up the long driveway to the Hall.

At the tradesman's door, Tom waited to see the housekeeper. The cook was clearing the kitchen from breakfast and asked him in out of the now falling rain.

'Come in, come in,' she said kindly. 'No use getting all wet through when there's shelter at hand. Sit you down over there out of my way for the housekeeper could keep you waiting a while.'

She was a large woman and Thomas could hear her breathing as she bustled round the kitchen piling dishes she had used by the sink for the scullery maid to wash up. The housekeeper was so long that Thomas had downed a pint of ale and a crust of bread and cheese by the time she came, with a chinking of keys on her belt, into the kitchen.

Thomas stood up and touched his forelock. He asked if there was any work for his sister who was a good worker. The housekeeper, a tall austere looking woman with her grey hair pulled back in a tight bun and wearing a long, black worsted gown replied that there was a position in the laundry room for mending and asked if she was neat with her needle.

'She is a fine needlewoman,' said Thomas and showed her a darn that she had made on his sock the evening before. He held up his foot and the housekeeper bent and scrutinised it then stood up. She seemed satisfied.

'Provided you can vouch that she is clean about her person and reliable with her time keeping, I will give her a month's trial. She can start on the first of next month but the position does not provide for her to live in.' The housekeeper hurried off and left Tom standing, cap in hand. He had meant to ask about shelter for Amy and the children but had not found the opportunity before the housekeeper had left the kitchen. He thanked the cook for her hospitality and went out into the rain.

He pulled up his collar and pushed his hands deep into his pockets as he retraced his steps down the long drive. The gatekeeper saw him approach through the window of the gatehouse and came to the door to ask if he had had success.

'Aye, for a job but I still have lodging for her and the bairns to see to,' said Tom and waved goodbye to the man and thanked him for his concern. During the long walk back to the farm he deliberated on the problem. Perhaps Amy and the children could have the room that he had been offered at the head gardener's cottage and he could find somewhere for himself. The more he thought on it, the better the idea seemed to him. He turned back and made his way through the torrential rain until he came to the cottage. The head gardener's wife was baking bread and wiping the dough from her fingers, opened the door at his knock.

'Why Thomas, come in, come in out of the rain. Why, you are soaked to the skin. Come here and sit alongside the fire and take off that wet coat. My husband will be back soon for his dinner.' The kindly woman fussed over him only returning to her kneading when she was sure that he was comfortable.

'You are very kind, Mrs Turner. I have a big favour to beg of you and your husband but should wait until he is here to ask it.'

'Why no Thomas. You have me all a curious. Can you not ask it now and we will repeat it when he is here?'

'You know the circumstance in which we find ourselves at the farm?' he began.

She nodded and sat herself in a chair on the other side of the fireplace.

'I have found work up at the Hall for Amy but am still at a loss for her lodging and that of the children. I was wondering if you would be good enough to take them for lodgers instead in the room that you have kindly offered to me, for I can sleep anywhere but I must see Amy and the children comfortably housed. I will pay my wage to you each week for your trouble Mrs Turner if you would be willing to put up with them.' Thomas looked at the good woman's face, his own grey with worry and fatigue.

'Concern yourself no more Thomas. I cannot think of a thing that would please me more. To have those little ones running about the house will cheer the old place up without a doubt and fill my lonely days a treat. I know that Mr Turner will feel the same way about it.' She took Thomas' proffered hand and patted it warmly. 'The room is small and they will be somewhat crowded together, but it is warm and dry up there over the kitchen.' She got up and went to the dresser, foraging in the cupboard underneath. She stood up and dusted off some books she had found. 'I even have some books from which I can begin to teach them their letters. See! They are full of brightly coloured pictures and will amuse the little ones for hours.'

The door opened and the head gardener came in shaking his coat from the rain.

'Thomas, my man. It is good to see you.' Before Thomas could speak a word, Mrs Turner had started to explain his visit and talk excitedly about the prospect. Mr Turner was as delighted as his wife until his face became suddenly serious and his hand went up to stop her.

'But what of Thomas? We are about to cast a soldier who is maimed by fighting for his country and has done all in his power to settle his entire family in work and lodging, out into the snow.' He said with great drama in his voice.

Mrs Turner's hands went up to her face aghast.

'You are right, husband. How could we be so thoughtless!'

'There is a small barn to the rear of this property, Thomas. It is at present full of bits and pieces of my gardening requirements but we could clear it, you and I, and take what we need up to the Hall and house it there. We could make the place, which is dry at least, as quarters for you as best we can and you can take your meals here with us and warm yourself by the fire here until it is time for bed. What do you think? Can it be done?'

'I have slept in far worse situations on the battlefield. I would thank you both and be glad of it.'

'That's settled then. And Amy's husband can visit her of an evening for you will all be in the same neck of the woods.' he laughed with pleasure.

15

As Thomas at last returned that evening, the relief on Amy's face was great and when he told them what had transpired during his absence she and Charles were amazed and delighted. They made plans to leave the farm on one evening when William was at the inn, saying nothing of their whereabouts or employment for in his present frame of mind, he might damage their intentions.

Meanwhile, William, ignorant of those intents continued to relish the thought of their final banishment with no notion as to how he would manage without them. All he could think of was the ultimate ownership of the farm and how he would appear before his friends, a landowner and man of property. All the proceeds from the living would be in his own pocket and no longer shared with feeding and clothing a family of which he had no use or interest. He was obsessed with the prospect which occupied his every waking hour.

So it was a shock to him when he arrived back at the farm one evening to find no light in the kitchen, no fire in the grate and worse, no supper on the table. He stood transfixed staring about him at the empty room, his anger growing by the moment. He ran up the stairs to the bedrooms to find them stripped and empty, then back down again to rant and rave about the kitchen, turning over chairs in his way and casting dishes to break on the floor.

His anger spent, he sank down on a chair by the ashes in the fireplace and huddled into his coat realising that not only had his pleasure at eviction been denied him but that this was how the house would be from this day hence.

In the morning after fitful sleep, he went down and found some cheese in the pantry that Amy had left, unable to bring herself to leave him without, drank from the milk pitcher and went out to the barn to start work. A hollow feeling in his stomach persisted as he realised his loneliness and he took his feelings out on old Dexter, beating him with a stick when he would not stand to be tacked up.

After a week had gone by, his plight became intolerable and he took into employment a girl from a nearby village to housekeep for him. She was a simple girl, plain and unkempt in her person but she could cook well enough even though her habits were dirty and the house looked little better after her so-called cleaning than it had before she started it. There was gossip at the inn that she should live in the farm alone with William, she a maid and he a single man but he paid no heed to it. As long as his supper was on the table when he came in from the fields and he could go to the inn with no complaint, he was for the time being, content.

As time went by, the farm became too much for him and he had to leave some fields barren. He sold off some sheep and cattle and drank the proceeds in a matter of weeks. His drinking was his one solace, for his life was not content and there was no joy in it.

One night, after an evening of drinking with his raucous friends, he tumbled in through the door to find his young housekeeper washing her hair before the fire. Her bodice was unlaced and pulled off her shoulders to keep from getting wet and in his drunken state, she appeared the most alluring of creatures. The poor simple girl had no defence against his unwelcome advances and when he pushed her back onto the table top sweeping the dishes from it with his arm, she could only scream in desperation but there was no one to hear her voice for miles around.

It became William's habit to take the girl on his return from the inn when in drink for she held no attraction for him at any other time. He paid her in little gifts for her silence but when she fell for a child, he knew that he would be forced to marry her and he beat her senseless in his fury and frustration. She was too frightened to go to her parents in her condition so within the month, they were married and her fate was sealed.

He was now a land-owner and a husband; a man of property across the board. It seemed to William that these facts should command some respect from his friends and neighbours. But they did not.

Backs were turned as he entered the inn and on most nights, he drank alone staring moodily at the groups of men he used to call friends as they laughed and roistered and gambled the night away. He had been one of their number until recently and he felt great anger that they should feel themselves qualified to judge him. They were little more than labourers on their father's land, accepting whatever pocket money it behove him to give them.

As to the older men. They could go hang with their principles and their self-righteous attitude. You did not get on in this world by hanging back and doffing your cap. You took what was yours and defended it and built it up until it was twice – three times what it was before.

The more William thought, the more his chest swelled with the anger within it and he banged down his fist on the table, upsetting his glass and spilling its contents on the wooden floor.

'At last, I have your attention,' he said standing up unsteadily.

'Sit down Blackwell, for you're full of drink and will fall over,' said one of his former friends, leaning on the bar and laughing with the others at William's red face.

'Yes, I'm drunk, but sober enough to notice when I am being cold shouldered. I told you all that within the year I would be a man of property and you scoffed. And now that I am, I believe it to be jealousy and envy that causes this treatment of me.'

'That farm of yours will be barren e'er long and you'll have nothing to show for your 'takeover of power,' said one young man saying the last phrase in a mocking tone.

'Tis one thing taking on property,' said an older man, a near neighbour of the Blackwells, 'but another in the way that you took it. Turning out your own brother and sister and her family with bairns and all? Tis a hard man with no heart that can do such a thing and a hard man with no heart cannot manage land and animals for he'll have no feel for it.'

'You don't know what you're talking about, you old fool. I was born on that farm and have grown up with it.'

'Aye but with your father's blood in your veins. I'd rather have water in mine.' And the young man laughed with his mates and held up his glass for another pint of ale in it.

William sprang at him but in his dazed state, missed his target and lay sprawled on the floor in the saw-dust and spit. In seconds, he found himself man-handled by the landlord and some others and he was flat on his back in the road in front of the inn with the door closed to him.

16

Charlie began work with twenty or so men who had come over from Ireland, engaged as labourers. For the most part they were thick set and heavily muscled, used to this kind of work, digging out for the new canals. But there were one or two that had come to England to find work only and like Charlie, had not been used to the demands that the groundwork required. These few, together with Charlie, suffered all manner of aches and pains from the long hours of digging and for a while, all Charlie could do was to fall on his truckle bed after the evening meal and sleep until morning light when the foreman woke him again.

Thomas saw him from time to time but it was just to wave and then back to work, for the foreman had a schedule to keep to and they were already behind. Thomas was just learning the ropes with the head gardener and his work was much lighter and with far less pressure. The pay was in proportion to the demands though and Charlie would make a nice nest egg if he could stand the pace, while Thomas would barely keep himself on his meagre stipend. But money isn't everything and his days were full of interest and instruction from the head gardener and Mr Turner was an excellent teacher. Thomas found himself greatly taken up with the subject and was a quick learner.

Amy was pleased with her job at the Hall and walked up with Tom every morning, stood to wave at her husband and then went in to the warmth and comfort of the laundry room.

She would glance out of the window from time to time in the hope that she would see Charlie passing below, wheeling a wheel barrow or with a pick over his shoulder but she seldom did. She missed him so much, both beside her in bed and his company to talk to. She would sit in the Turner's parlour of an evening, the children in bed and Tom smoking his pipe and chatting with Mr Turner and Mrs Turner with her knitting or mending, telling of all the amusing things that the children had done during the day and she would think of poor Charlie in a long line of truckle beds with the sleeping navvies and just their snoring for company. He would be too tired to feel the cold but not too tired to feel the loneliness.

They had heard that William had taken a bride and that he had not mended his ways, also that the farm was going downhill fast. One evening, Thomas had taken a walk towards the farmland and had seen two fields had not been planted but lay fallow and full of weeds. He had turned back, not wishing to bump into William on his way to the inn and walked up the slope to the pasture where the sheep were scattered. They were not well cared for and several were limping from foot rot and all with last year's fleece still on their backs, clogged with mud. He shook his head sadly and made his way back to the cottage. As he approached, he saw Amy pass the window. The curtains were not drawn and the light from the candles in the kitchen and the parlour fanned out from the windows in a pool of warm yellow light in the little front garden, full of mixed flowers and vegetables. He stood for a while looking at the scene within, the children in their night gowns, a glass of milk in each little pair of hands as they sat, one on each of Mr Turner's knees as he turned over the pages of a book; Mrs Turner beaming at her husband with a sock to be mended on a wooden mushroom in her hand; Amy walking backwards and forwards between the two rooms, clearing the supper things and folding the children's clothes for the morning. Her face was bearing the sadness of separation but looking well otherwise, for they lacked for nothing. He did not like to disturb them so went straight to his bed in the barn to think of all the things on his mind.

The months went by, winter came and went and Charlie had grown strong and used to the work. The Irishmen were, for the most part, good company and he had made some friends amongst them. They were worse off than he for their families were across the water and they didn't see them for months on end, while he was now able to go to see Amy and the children once a week on a Sunday and spend a pleasant hour or two with them. The promise of this visit kept him going throughout the week.

William's wife, Donna had had her baby, a girl and they both flourished in her ignorance of anything that could go wrong. She muddled through the day, rushing from one job to another and rarely completing anything she started. She would be in trouble from William for not having his supper on the table and next find that she had not washed the baby's nappies and would have to use a torn up sheet for the job. She would put out the washing at night on the hedges and find it blown across the yard by morning and have to wash it all over again. But her empty head gave her no trouble and she was mostly in a pleasant mood now that she had a baby to play with.

William grew more and more dour as time went on. He had no friends, an imbecile for a wife, a mewling baby girl and a farm that was all work and less and less return for his labour. Old Dexter had died in his traces and he had been forced to fork out for a new horse to take his place. It was a fight each day to get the animal to do his bidding and he realised how fortunate he had been, for old Dexter knew his job and practically walked the plough on his own. He knew he would have to take on a labourer but was loath to pay the wage he would need to get a man to live in at the farm.

He muddled on, leaving more and more of the land untended then took on a man who came to the door for work. The fellow stayed for a week, picked up his wages and a number of tools belonging to the farm and was not seen again.

The next man he employed was better and worked under William's direction but was slow about it. With his help, the farm picked up a little but the fields had lain fallow for too long and to get even one of them back to cultivation was hard, back-breaking work. William fought the new cart horse instead of encouraging him and when the ploughshare was broken by misuse, William used his whip to the horse in his vexation. The great horse turned on him and reared up, towering over the stocky little man. Poised in the air as William lifted his whip again, the animal brought his weight to bear down on this human irritation. He was still tethered to the plough and as he pranced and whinnied and flailed with his great feathered hooves, part of the sharp curve of the blade caught William on the side of his body and tossed him into the air and then to the ground like a rag doll. The horse finally broke free and galloped away up the field, leaving William bleeding and crushed in the furrow.

It was evening before William dragged himself to the farmhouse, clutching his side and dragging the broken leg. The white bone stuck clear out of his torn trouser leg and his shoulder was misshapen by dislocation. Blood was caked in his hair and down his face from the cut on his head and he looked at death's door.

Donna shrieked when she saw him and almost dropped the baby. Ben, the hired man, came running from the barn where he had been occupied all day when he heard her cries.

'God Almighty, Mr Blackwell. What has happened to you?'

'Don't stand there the pair of you. Run for the doctor, Ben, and be sharp about it.' He sank into the chair at the side of the fire and fainted away.

The doctor set his leg in a splint the best he could and stitched up the torn flesh round it and along the side of his body. Stitches were needed in the head wound as well and re-locating his shoulder sent William into a dead faint again.

'He is in a bad way Mrs Blackwell,' said the doctor after he had worked for two solid hours. 'There are no two bones about it,' he continued not realising the aptness of his expression. 'All I can recommend is sleep and nourishment if he will take it. His leg will never be right even if it does not take the gangrene which is common in such cases. If that happens I will be forced to take off the leg. But we shall see, we shall see. He is a strong man and stands as good a chance as any. Time will tell. I will visit again in five day's time and pass judgement. Good night.'

William was in fever by the following morning and Donna flapped about him not knowing what to do for the best, so doing nothing. He became delirious and shouted and cursed from his bed then fell into deep sleep breathing noisily. When the doctor returned on the morning of the fifth day he was most concerned and doubted that he could save the leg never mind the patient. He applied leeches and poultices to the affected areas and said he would return two days hence.

The following morning after a further night of delirium, William seemed to rally and sleep more easily and by the time the doctor returned the next day, was much improved and had eaten some porridge for his breakfast.

'Well I thought we had lost you, William,' said the doctor in a cheerful voice.

'You may as well have done for the use I will be from now on,' growled William. 'This farm will be the death of me.'

'Come come, my man. That was a nasty accident and all but the leg are showing signs of healing well. There is no sign yet of gangrene in it and if that remains the case, you will have got off lightly.'

'And will it bear my weight again?'

'We shall have to see when you are well enough to test it, William.'

'That horse is mad and will be shot for this. I will not have him near me again.'

'He looked a fine animal when I saw him in the yard. It seems a pity to blame him for an – accident,' said the doctor diplomatically, having seen the whip marks on the horses flank and shoulders.

'He has the devil in him and I'll not abide him. I will shoot him myself as soon as I am able.'

The doctor nodded and went downstairs.

'He is on the mend Mrs Blackwell and threatening all manner of revenge on the poor horse. It is a good sign for him but not so for the horse. Perhaps you can dissuade him when he is well enough to come down and in a more even temper.'

'Oh, he don't listen to me doctor. I keeps me mouth shut.'

'Well that's as may be. I will send you my bill but you must call me if the patient worsens.'

William continued to improve each day and with the improvement came a frustration and anger that even Donna had not seen in him before. He tossed and turned in his bed and banged on the floor with a stick every five minutes demanding this or that attention; a drink or some food or a fresh pillow. Donna relied heavily on Ben, the hired man to bring a rabbit or kill a chicken for her and she muddled through well enough.

News of the accident eventually reached Thomas' ears and he told Amy what had happened. She determined to go and see what she could do to help and the following Sunday walked to the farm with a basket of baking and fruit.

William was down in the kitchen sitting by the fire with a blanket round his knees when she knocked on the door.

'Come in if you're going to,' growled William from his chair.

'It is me, Amy,' she said coming in and placing the basket upon the table.

'It's you, come to gloat I suppose.'

'Of course not William. I would not wish this on you. I have brought some provisions for you.'

'You can take them back. I'll have none of your charity here. We have no need of help from the likes of you. This is my place and you are not welcome so you can get out and ... and don't come back.' He was shouting now and the effort was clearly exhausting him.

'If that is what you want, William, I will go but I'll leave these for Donna and the baby.' Amy patted the basket and left appalled at the state in which she had found her little brother.

William's leg healed but did not support him well enough to walk and he was forced to rely on a crutch and two pieces of wood strapped with leather round his leg. He kept to his word and shot the horse in the head as soon as he was able to hold a gun. The hired man kept the farm from grinding to a halt but there was barely a living to be had from it. The stock was sold and much of the farm machinery, the hay store from the loft had all but gone and so too the straw. William could not walk the distance to the inn and Donna was sent to buy supplies so that William could drink himself into a stupor in his own kitchen. Soon, he could not pay the hired man who left, still owed two month's wages.

Without him, Donna could not manage. There was no cow to milk for the baby and no meat save a side of bacon from the last pig to be slaughtered that hung, fly-blown and black from the rafters. If she went near William he would catch hold of her and try to slap her but she was well able to side-step him in his state and even that small pleasure was denied him. When she had dug the last of the vegetables from the patch and stewed them to a pulp on a fire made with the last of the wood she could find by the barn, she determined to leave and go back to her parents, She dare not tell William but got up early one morning while he was still in bed, wrapped her few belongings in a shawl strapped round her waist and with the babe in her arms, took to the road. He never saw her again.

17

It was several weeks before William's body was found by a passing foreign man hawking for work. He had knocked on the farm door and receiving no reply searched the farm buildings for a sign of life. He found instead, a dead man in the barn pierced by a harrow beneath the broken boards of the hay loft and gnawed by rats so that the blackened face was barely recognisable. He went to the next farm he came to and tried in his broken English to make them understand what he had found. Thinking he had killed William Blackwell, the poor man was seized and held captive until the magistrate was called. But the magistrate, when he arrived, was able to make more sense of the fellow and together the neighbour, the magistrate and his men went to the Blackwell farm to discover for themselves the rotting body of William Blackwell.

The magistrate backed away from the stinking form. 'The Lord has his own way of passing judgement and retribution,' he said with a handkerchief over his nose.

There were 'Ayes' from those gathered there all reluctant to stand near or by the body.

William was buried near his father, a verdict of accidental death having been proclaimed by the magistrate. It was concluded that William had climbed into the loft and in tearing up the boards for firewood, had fallen through onto the spike of the harrow. Only the family attended the funeral and no gathering followed the occasion.

The family did not at once move back to the farm for Charlie had contracted to finish the job at the Hall and his final payment fell due only when the work was completed. Amy decided to stay on with her work there which she enjoyed and was profitable while Mrs Turner continued to mind the children. Thomas was first to leave reluctantly, as he had enjoyed the gardening job and had learned a great deal from working with Mr Turner, the head gardener, under his tutelage.

Thomas said goodbye to a tearful Mrs Turner early in the spring, for the work on the farm would begin in earnest and he had to start at the earliest opportunity. He hired a youngster, Harry to help him, the son of a neighbour and together they began the enormous task of restoring the farm. Once seed and a horse and plough had been acquired, all Thomas' money was spent, but it was a start and Amy came each Sunday with provisions and baking, some of it gifts from the Hall kitchen. She cleaned the windows and washed and mended the torn curtains and scrubbed the kitchen table top and gathered dry sticks for the fire then left, tired but satisfied, to return to the cottage and her children.

Thomas and young Harry worked from dawn till dusk and good neighbours lent whatever tools they could spare to help the enterprise. Chickens were brought to fill the hen houses and provide meat and eggs and a piglet arrived one Sunday morning squealing its small pink head off as its owner struggled to hold it under his arm. The gifts were all the more valued and appreciated for the sacrifice they had caused the neighbours who were not themselves wealthy people.

Summer came and the yard was alive with the busy clucking and scratching of the chickens and the snorting of the growing pig who, without a sty to live in, happily wandered the yard and barns and grubbed in the old vegetable patch, still unplanted for want of time. The house was clean if un-repaired and Thomas was a moderately able cook for him and Harry. Some of the fields were now planted and the weather was kind enough to speed the new growth. As soon as there was some respite from the field work, Thomas and Harry set to to repair the barns and stables, for stock came before home comfort in farming life and the new carthorse, Dolly, was of major importance to the running of a good farm and must be treated accordingly. Good treatment would give good return. The chicken run was the next job in hand, for the chickens laid eggs wherever they fancied and gathering them was time consuming. Proper laying boxes and protection at night was beneficial. The pig had grown used to roaming free so it was decided to fence the vegetable patch against him for future planting and leave him his pleasure. It was too late for vegetables this season but the ground could benefit from some good rotted horse manure which would break down over the winter.

One Sunday, Charlie accompanied Amy and the children to the farm for a visit and was amazed at the progress Thomas and Harry together had made. Mr and Mrs Turner came too and brought with them enough food for a Sunday feast with cold roast beef, cold, cooked vegetables which they fried over the fire and an apple pie and cream for pudding. Afterwards, they sat round the fire talking and planning the future, all that is, except Charlie and Amy who went for a walk together up to the pasture, hand in hand.

18

The autumn came and went with the harvest, good but small, barely making enough to buy seed for the next year. Charlie's work at the Hall was coming to an end and he looked forward to the time when he could return to the farm and be with his family once more. Daisy now attended the village school and was a bright little pupil and little Tom was growing fast.

Amy loved her work at the Hall and decided she would stay on living now at the farm and managing the housework round it. Mrs Turner was a willing and eager child minder and little Tom was her pride and joy. Amy had made friends at work with the other girls and although the housekeeper was strict, she was fair and, provided they kept up with their work did not object to their chatting and laughter. The conversation, as with all young women together, often turned to the young men around them and one particular young groom would wave to them from the yard as they sat near a window. When they came to hang out the washing, he would make it his business to be near at hand and chat to them until he was called away.

Amy could not but notice the fluttering feeling in the pit of her stomach at the appearance of the young groom. He was tall and bronzed from the sun and had a clear complexion, almost girl like, with no facial hair. His leather waistcoat and tight groom's breeches showed a good physique and his hair was dark and curly like a gypsy's. Amy would linger just that little bit longer than the other girls over the washing line hardly knowing what ailed her. She found out that his name was George and that he was twenty three, the same age as herself.

George noticed the girl called Amy and although he knew that she was the only married girl amongst the bunch from the laundry room, she was certainly the prettiest and appeared to be interested in him. Always one to take the easiest route, George set his cap at Amy and made a pact with himself that he would have her before midsummer day or eat his hat.

And so it was in that spring while Tom was struggling to restore the farm and Charlie was slaving in the Italian garden and Mrs Turner was looking after little Tom while Daisy went to school, that Amy allowed her romantic feelings full rein and her responsibilities and good sense to fly out of the laundry room window. She mooned over the pretty young groom and as with all young secret lovers, she and George found ingenious ways of meeting despite the demands of their masters. When it was time each day to go home to the gardener's cottage to pick up the children, Amy and George would spend a furtive half hour walking hand in hand along the edge of the Hall farm fields close by the tall hedges.

Mrs Turner noticed the change in Amy and also the lateness of the hour that she came home. Amy would have a dreamy look and seemed unable to converse sensibly. She was flushed and her hair tousled and often her shoes muddied when the road was clear. Mrs Turner came to one conclusion and spoke of her fears to Mr Turner.

'I am sure that Amy has fallen for a young man at the Hall. Poor girl. She had no youthful romances and no dreams like most young women. I understand her weakness in this case but I am sure that she loves Charlie and has for the moment forgotten it.'

'The family has had nothing but misery to deal with and Thomas and Charlie are working so hard that I'm loath to confront them with yet another problem,' said Mr Turner shaking his head.

'But Mr Turner, I fear if this situation is left, it will become serious and Amy will suffer as well.'

'What would you have me do, mother? Would it not be better for you to speak to Amy and make her see sense?' said her husband.

'It takes two to make a romance and the young man must be aware that Amy is a married woman with children.'

Mr and Mrs Turner decided that each of them would speak, he to the groom and she to Amy and try to make them see the folly of their ways.

It was a warm May evening when Amy and George having finished their day's work, crept through the ornamental rose garden, dodging behind the huge topiary yews if they saw any one and finally across the little bridge over the stream to the hedge that bordered the Hall pasture land. George was singing a little song under his breath as he sucked on a length of grass and felt the warm evening breeze in his hair. Amy's hand was in his own and he had a good feeling that this evening was going to be lucky for him. Amy was putty in his hands.

Amy felt the warmth of his body against her arm and the grip of his hand on hers and an exciting feeling burst in her chest at the thought that he might kiss her again as he had a few days before. They did not look at each other but stared straight ahead afraid of the expressions they would see in each other's eyes. Suddenly, George turned and took Amy in his arms and their faces came together quite naturally and then, the kiss that Amy had longed for. This time it lasted long and

George's lips were eager and searching. The tiniest doubt crossed Amy's mind but she succumbed to the kiss and clung with her arms round George's body. Then he was pushing her down into the long grass beneath the hedge and his hands seemed everywhere on her body and she was pushing them off with her own. She did not want this. This was not right. It was too much like before when she was a girl. Charlie was not like this. Charlie was gentle and – exciting. This was not exciting. It was fearful.

Amy struggled from under George and struck his upturned face with her hand.

'Get off me. Get off me!' she shouted and scrambled up running along the hedge until she came to the gate. George did not follow her. Good God! There were easier fish in the sea than this! He rubbed his reddened face with the back of his hand, put on his cap and started back for the stables at the Hall, pulling the waistcoat and the shirt beneath it straight as he went.

Amy ran all the way to the cottage, the tears streaming down her face but no sound to accompany them. She was breathless when she reached the gate, but conscious that she must pull herself together before facing Mrs Turner. But Mrs Turner had watched her running up the lane from the kitchen window and sent the children into the back garden to play.

'So it has come to a head, has it my dear?' she said as Amy came through the door.

Amy glanced up innocently as though she did not understand the question.

'Come now Amy, dear. I know that something has been amiss with you for these past weeks and if I am not mistaken, there is a young man at the bottom of it?'

'Why I cannot think why you should imagine such a thing, Mrs Turner.' Amy's laugh was false.

'Amy, you have a good man in Charlie. Love does not always enter a marriage but it has in yours and you should treasure it. You have two beautiful children and your menfolk making a home for you. You're not rich but you want for nothing.'

Amy stared at her hands that lay in her lap, her thick, red hair hanging down and concealing her face. There was silence between them and then Mrs Turner noticed that Amy's shoulders were shaking and her hands were up to her eyes.

'Oh my dear,' she said holding out her arms for Amy. Amy fell into her arms sobbing.

'I thought I loved him. I forgot Charlie. I wanted to forget everything and start again and be young and pretty,' she cried.

'I know, I know,' soothed Mrs Turner stroking her hair.

'I can't go back to the Hall – I can't.'

'Perhaps it's best if you don't, Amy, and Amy… '

Amy looked into Mrs Turner's face with her own which was tear-stained.

'If you are thinking that you must admit what has happened to Charlie… ?'

'Yes, I must. There must be no secrets between us. We have always told each other everything and swore that was how it would be.'

'No Amy. Some things are best left unsaid. How can it benefit your relationship to hurt Charlie? It is more often we tell something that we are ashamed of so that some of the burden is taken from our own shoulders and rests on our loved ones. No! This burden you must carry alone. It is your punishment, if you like. Charlie does not deserve to have to bear it. But, my dear, do not make too much of it. It was a young mistake and many besides you have fallen for it in the past and many more in the future. Do you love Charlie?'

'Yes, I do,' said Amy without hesitation. 'He is my friend, my father, my brother and my dear husband.'

'I am most pleased to hear you put 'friend' at the head of your list, Amy, for that is a most important component of a marriage. Now dry your eyes and go and collect your little ones.'

*

Mr Turner finished his work in the knot garden and wandered up to the stables before picking up his coat to go home. He knew where he was going because he had seen Amy and George come out from behind a yew tree and make towards the little bridge over the stream that very afternoon. George was whistling in the far stable while brushing out the mane on the master's horse. He glanced up when the head gardener approached.

'You're a little off your beat, are you not? The garden sheds are that way. You've no business in here unless you've come for horse shit,' laughed George.

Mr Turner grasped George by his coat collars and swung him round to face him, his face close to George's.

'You're a cocky young man and no mistake but I'll tell you one thing – if you come near or by to Amy Marriot or touch a hair of her head, you'll have nothing to be cocky with for I'll relieve you of that appendage with my own two hands. Do you understand?' Mr Turner's face was very red and his teeth gritted tight together so that he hissed the words through them.

George pulled himself free and shook himself.

'I've no use for the girl anyway. There are plenty of pretty girls that would be glad of my company,' he said but kept his distance, half shielded by the horse.

Mr Turner turned to go, 'Then set your cap at them but be sure that they are not wed.'

19

It was true as Mrs Turner had said that Amy's guilt lay heavy on her heart but as the days at the farm went by and the routine settled back into place, the episode of her infatuation was pushed further and further back until it became unreal and more like a romantic dream she had experienced. Charlie was soon to finish at the Hall and would come home with a tidy sum of money, more than most of the other men because he had not frittered away his wages on drink each week and would have the savings to add to the end bonus.

He longed to be back at the farm with Amy and the children, still only able to see them fleetingly on Sundays. Thomas and young Harry had made great strides towards the recovery of the farm but he knew that his financial input would make a great difference to their struggle as well as his own pair of hands. He felt overwhelmingly, the desire he had for Amy but sensed a returning shyness, perhaps coldness, in her behaviour towards him that concerned him. He had heard rumours amongst the lads at work of one of the grooms being taken to task because of his advances towards a young woman from the laundry and this, plus the fact that Amy had left the work at the Hall suddenly when he was sure she had enjoyed it, gave him grounds for concern. He could confront Amy and risk seeming to accuse her of something she may not have done. He could ask at the Hall and people would know that he didn't trust his own wife. What he could not do was decide what to do. The thing hung between them like a curtain; not impenetrable but a barrier just the same. He could not talk to Tom for he clearly had no knowledge of it and would naturally consider his sister in need of defence and yet, the possibility of Amy's disloyalty continued to fester because it did not have an airing.

Charlie contrived to meet Mr Turner one afternoon in the Hall gardens on some pretext regarding tools from the barn.

'Why hello, Charlie, my man. How goes it with you?' said Mr Turner in his usual amiable way.

'I am well enough Mr Turner,' he replied. 'There is something though that is troubling me that you might be able to throw some light upon.'

Mr Turner knew at once to what he referred but hoped he was mistaken. 'Why, fire away, Charlie. Fire away.'

'It is regarding Amy. There are some rumours... I am sure that.... perhaps you have heard something?'

'Charlie, come sit beside me on this log. I've a mind to smoke a pipe of tobacco.' Charlie's palms became cold and clammy but he did as he as was asked and sat down while Mr Turner lit his pipe painfully slowly.

'Charlie, do you love Amy?' he began rather unexpectedly.

'I have always loved her, yes, and still do,' he replied.

'There are things in this world that are sent to test us, to try out our resolve. The family that you married into has had more than its fair share of tests, Charlie. I think you'll agree?'

'I do,' said Charlie simply.

'Charlie, I know about the rumours and Amy's personal trial. I am not a religious man, Charlie but I can tell you that Amy was tested and was tempted by some power beyond our understanding. She went to my wife and told her of her troubles and that she resisted the young man's advances and my wife believes her, as do I. I myself spoke to the young man involved, an impudent and cocky individual and he has taken himself off, with a little help from his superiors at the Hall, to cause trouble in some other part of the land.

'Amy is a good woman, wife and mother. She has had a difficult life but she knows she can depend on you to love her unconditionally. Don't rock that love by bringing forth something that is done and over with, Charlie. You have been apart for a long time and your mission now is to build your relationship with your family to the strength it had before, slowly but surely.'

'I thank you for your intervention in this matter which I shall not speak of again. You are right, of course, and I shall take your advice. You and your wife have been the mother and father of this family that we have sadly lacked, the grandparents to my children that they will always remember.'

20

Two years passed and the farm thrived on hard work and a good business head on Tom's shoulders. Little Tom was always to be found at Thomas' side, aping everything he did, many a time when he should have been at school. Daisy, still as pretty as a picture, was an especially gifted pupil and aspired to be a teacher when she was full grown. Strange as it should be, there was a special relationship between her and Charlie. Amy was a few months into her third pregnancy and was not well with it. Charlie put it down to the fact that Amy missed her mother with her through her time and he may well have been right, but the Turners were frequent visitors and Mrs Turner kept her buoyant. Neither Charlie nor Amy had ever mentioned the business of her affair with George, though Amy had found it easier to push to the back of her mind than Charlie had. Long hours walking the plough alone or stacking the stooks of ripened corn gave him too much time to think but as time went by and Amy was such a loving wife, he realised the wisdom of Mr Turner's words; that love is a delicate flower that can too easily fade - but with time and nurturing can spring forth again from strong roots.

The doctor was needed at Amy's confinement for it was a difficult breach birth and beyond Mrs Turner's experience, more limited than Amy's mother's had been. The baby was a healthy boy but Amy had to suffer some surgery and she and Charlie were told that there would be no more children. Amy was a long time recovering her strength and Charlie and Tom were worried to death. Mrs Turner stayed in the house and nursed her as if she were her own daughter. But Amy was inherently strong and once the baby was weaned early and did not drain her of strength, she began to get better.

The fine years of clement weather and good husbandry established the farm's output. The pastures were grazed by a fine herd of a new breed of sheep that Tom had brought in, less prone to foot rot and yielding twin lambs more often than single. The milking herd was kept small for easy management and concentration went on pigs, housed on the low fields, farthest from the marsh leachings. Charlie had planted a small orchard of plumbs and damsons and Amy looked after a regiment of vegetables lined up against the house.

Charlie and Thomas planned to build a new barn for straw storage and early lambing on the east side of the yard that would complete three sides of a square and shield the house from the prevailing wind in the winter. They began the work soon after harvest when the money began to come in from the grain. It was a big project for just two men but they had tackled as much in the past and they knew they would have support from the neighbours when they could spare the time.

Thomas had met a young widow when in town one market day and had begun to visit her at her aunt's house where she lodged with her small daughter. When he admitted as much, shyly to Amy and Charlie one evening, they were delighted and said so. Each evening after work he would walk to the town and spend time with his new love and talks of marriage were in the air. The autumn came and then the winter and with it, the bad weather. Thomas would return home at night, sometimes wet to the skin and Amy was worried about the strain on him after a hard day's work for he was no longer a young man.

'It would be so good for Thomas to marry and I would dearly love to see him settled for if anyone deserves it, he does,' she said to Charlie one evening as they sat alongside the fire. The wind was blowing hard and the rain was loud against the window pains. She shivered at the thought of Thomas being out on such a night.

'I'm sure he would ask her to marry him if there was room enough here for them all,' she went on. 'It would help at least if we could afford a riding horse for him, don't you think, Charlie?'

'I have been as concerned as you are about his welfare and giving it much thought. I would much prefer to put the money for a horse towards building him a small cottage nearby. We have money set aside for more pigs, but I consider that we should delay buying in more in favour of a cottage.'

'Oh Charlie, that would be so good. We would be quite the little family group and I would so appreciate the company.' Amy was excited at the project. 'Let's put it to Thomas the moment he comes in.'

It was late – soon after midnight when Thomas arrived home soaked to the skin. He was shivering and feverish with flushed cheeks and beads of sweat under the rim of his hat. Amy's concern showed itself in fretfulness that he should be out on such a night and she helped him off with his coat, chiding him all the while.

'Go up and take off all those wet clothes and put on dry and I will have hot milk and brandy ready when you come downstairs.' Thomas protested that he would rather get straight into bed but Amy would not hear of it, insisting that he should have the drink inside him before he slept. Charlie shrugged as if to show his sympathy but that nothing would satisfy Amy but that Thomas should comply. Amy busied herself with the hot milk and poured a good measure of brandy into it as Thomas came back down rubbing his wet hair with a towel.

'Come sit by the fire and drink this, for we have something to put to you. Charlie.'

Charlie put their ideas to him as he sat shivering and hugging the mug to warm his hands. Thomas was as delighted as his condition would allow and they determined that the work would start as soon as the weather would allow. Thomas confided in them that he would propose marriage on his very next visit and they all three took a tot of brandy to celebrate.

The following morning was dark with grey cloud-filled skies that promised snow. It was not raining but the temperature had plummeted and frost was on the inside of the windows. The puddles in the yard had a thin coating of ice and the animals and fowl had stayed inside their houses. Even the cock had not crowed his morning overture.

Charlie was out fetching wood for the fire and Amy dressed the children in their warmest clothes before they came down. She went in to Thomas to find him with a high fever, unable to get warm despite the extra blankets that Amy had put over him.

'You'll not be rising today Tom. You must stay there and sweat this fever out.' she insisted. Thomas protested but she pushed him back down under the blankets and he had no more strength to oppose her.

The snow came in the late afternoon and settled its silent blanket on top of the frozen mud. Amy had kept the children from school and Charlie had spent the day feeding the animals and putting down deep bedding for them. He brought in a chicken for Amy to make supper and a broth for Thomas, and then went back out to chop wood and stack in the barn.

Thomas' fever broke that night after Amy had sat with him, bathing his forehead as he tossed and turned. Charlie made up a bed for him in the kitchen and stacked wood on the fire to last most of the night and together they helped Thomas down the stairs. He slept as soon as he was settled there and Amy and Charlie went to bed with a feeling of some relief.

In the morning Thomas showed signs of recovery and was able to take some broth and later, some bread and cheese but was still very weak.

The snow stayed for several days, replenished every now and then by fresh flurries and Thomas worried that his absence would cause concern to Mary, his future wife. But there was no help for it for the roads were impassable and all business at a standstill. The situation was good for Thomas, in that it gave him time to build up his strength and with the knowledge that he was not causing problems for Charlie.

As the snow began to thaw, the rivers became swollen and flooding was feared. Thomas was now up and about and insisted that he help Charlie to get the animals onto higher ground. The work was heavy in the deep mud left by the retreating snow. The two men had to manhandle the pig shelters from the low fields up to the higher pastures and bring the pregnant sheep down to the barn for lambing and shelter. They toiled for long hours and well after dark to complete the task before the low fields finally flooded, and no sooner had they finished than the lambing began in earnest and they were up all night in the barn. Thankfully, the farm and yard were above the flood water line and Amy was able to take food across to the barn and warm drinks to sustain the two men.

The work was backbreaking but rewarding in that most of the new breed yielded twin lambs.

After two long weeks, the waters began to retreat back within the broken banks of the river leaving the flotsam and debris in their wake and a thick grey mud where grass had once been. The swollen carcasses of animals from farms unable to find high enough ground for their animals lay where the waters had deposited them, while black crows pecked at their eyes and gaping mouths. Men from neighbouring farms came to help bury them but the mud made walking exhausting work and some slept in the barn with the sheep, too tired to go home to their beds at night. Amy was kept busy baking bread and frying bacon to sustain them and the children were under her feet unable to go out to play.

At last the sun played its warm rays on the men's backs and and as if by magic, green shoots appeared through the mud. The trees showed a bright green haze over their branches and here and there snowdrops carpeted the woodland floor. The pigs, untended during the flood, had managed, as pigs will, to grub enough sustenance from their new fields but had rendered the ground unusable for any other purpose and it was decided that they should remain there. Once the sheep were back on the pasture, there was time to stop and make plans for the spring. Thomas was eager to go to see Mary but he was not well. The heavy work and bad weather so soon after his fever had taken their toll and Thomas had visibly aged. A chesty cough troubled him and he would bang his chest with his fists to clear it when a bout of coughing was brought on by dust from the hay or smoke from the fire.

Amy was concerned about it and bought honey from a bee-keeping neighbour to make a soothing syrup for him, but the cough persisted and became much worse. One day, Amy glanced out of the kitchen window to see Thomas bent over in the yard coughing harshly. Then she saw blood come from his mouth that he wiped away with some grass he plucked and he heeled the tell tail marks under his shoe to conceal them before straightening up and taking deep gasping breaths of air. After he had recovered, he walked away to the barn not knowing that he had been seen.

Amy was sick with worry. She had heard of such symptoms and knew of only one outcome. She cried into Charlie's shoulder that night and he was barely able to understand her halting explanation.

'Aye, I have seen it,' he admitted, 'but thought best not to worry you about it. But the spring is ahead of us and the warmer weather will do nothing but good. I will make sure he has light work and stays away from the dust of the barn that always seems to set him off with his coughing. Best not to mention it to him. No use bringing the matter up when it is clear he would rather not speak of it. Now, go to sleep and remember that Tom is strong and has been through harder times than we can imagine in the war and come out of it. He will get better with the weather.' Charlie hugged Amy to him, hoping that his words would bring her comfort for he had little faith in them himself.

Thomas did improve a little with the better weather and Amy was able to push her concerns to the back of her mind and enjoy her family around her. She worked diligently in the vegetable patch and was rewarded with promising rows of tiny vegetables and salad plants. Charlie was forced to use all his ingenuity to keep Thomas from work in the dusty barn or heavy work that brought on the coughing. Nothing was said between them, either regarding the state of Thomas' health or the fact that he no longer visited the widow, Mary, or spoke of marrying her.

When June came and Amy's birthday, Charlie gave her some money to buy cloth for a new dress and Thomas gave her money for new shoes to go with it. She was delighted and went to town full of anticipation, imagining the sprigged muslin she would choose at Brown's, the haberdasher. Later, she was munching a little jam tart she had bought for her lunch and clutching her purchases under her arm when she bumped into Mary coming round a corner as pre-occupied as herself. Mary was a comely woman with rosy cheeks and a ready smile. She was not slim but neither was she fat but filled her skin in a pleasant roundness that prompted warm contact.

'Why Amy, how good to see you. You've been shopping I see,' said Mary, embracing her, 'How is Thomas?'

Amy paused, unable to decide how to answer her.

'It's all right Amy. I know about Thomas' illness. Come, let us go into the inn and sit and talk with a glass to refresh us and you can show me your purchases.'

The two women sat at a table by an open window for the air was always tainted with smoke, summer and winter alike, in the inn.

'Thomas is not too bad now that summer has come, and we are hoping for the best,' said Amy, starting to open the brown paper that wrapped her new dress material and new shoes. After Mary had admired the contents of the parcel, she began to explain.

'Thomas came to me last winter. He told me that he had determined to ask me to marry him and that he was most fond of me. As you can imagine, I was pleased as punch for I had grown equally fond of him and little Ellie adored him. But then he told me of his coughing illness and how he was spitting blood. He was candid and said that most men and women died of this curse and that he would not make a widow of me again. He said it was best if he left me free to find another man and when I protested that he was the one I wanted whatever the outcome, he was adamant. He said we must part and if by chance, he survived the disease, he would return to find me if I was still free but that I was not to refuse another offer in the meantime.'

'Oh, Mary. I am so sorry for it. I was so looking forward to your company at the farm and Daisy and little Ellie would have grown up like sisters. But we must keep hopeful that all our plans will come to pass. Tom is not too bad and Charlie says his strength and fortitude saw him through the war and will see him through this, and my Charlie is always right.'

'I will wait, Amy, for there is no other man for me and if I can't have Thomas, I will have no one. You are fortunate in Charlie, Amy, for he is a good man. Let us hope that his prediction does not let us down.'

21

As soon as the dampness that accompanied the autumn came, Thomas' cough grew worse again. His chest became congested and Charlie had to hit his back to dislodge the collected matter in his lungs. The bouts of coughing exhausted him and his throat became raw and inflamed. Food was hard to swallow and Amy made stews all the time, pretending that the children loved them so much and she mashed Tom's vegetables to make it easy to get down.

Charlie called the doctor after one particularly bad night but the poor man had little to offer in advice more than they were doing already and went through the door shaking his head and taking no payment.

Amy nursed Thomas unstintingly through most of that winter and was filled with a strange relief when at last, in the January of the following year, he breathed his last, for he had suffered so much and with so little complaint.

Charlie and young Harry had managed well enough but Charlie saw how much the strain had ebbed away Amy's resolve and humour. She was so thin and so pale and all the friends that had come to bid Thomas their respect at his funeral remarked on how much it had taken from her. The gathering at the funeral was great in number for Thomas had made many friends and was well liked. Mr and Mrs Turner were towers of strength to Amy and Charlie and Mrs Turner looked after the three children, having arranged for neighbours to help with the spread after the burial. Thomas was buried in a grave beside his mother on the far side of the cemetery from her husband and William, a most unusual arrangement but all that Amy would agree to in her distress at Thomas' death and her mother's three years before.

The little kitchen and parlour were filled with friends and neighbours who lingered long at these events, funerals and weddings, for they were almost the only social occasions in this hard-working community. Gradually, the numbers dwindled and by nightfall, only the Turners and Charlie, Amy and the sleeping children remained. Little Tom was unable to accept that his namesake uncle would never be at his side again and had only fallen asleep at last with exhaustion from sobbing his childish heart out.

Charlie made up the fire and the four sat round it each with his or her own thoughts.

'You've lost a good man there and no mistake,' said Mr Turner at last, breaking the silence.

'What you've got to think of is this, Charlie and Amy,' he went on. 'Most that went away from round these parts, to the war, never came back. Thankfully, Thomas did. Aye, he may have been maimed and blinded, but the man came back and you have had the pleasure of his company for more years than many folk with their loved ones that went for soldiers. He once told me of his anguish at having left you all, your mother, Amy and you, particularly and the guilt he felt. He called it 'running away'. But he was given time to make up for that guilt he felt rightly or wrongly. And no man could have tried harder, even though he had but one arm and one eye, to do that. I know myself how hard it was for him to garden as I directed but struggle as he might, he always completed the tasks I set him.'

He finished in a choking voice, 'I could not have loved him better, been more proud, had he been my own son.' His voice trailed away and his wife went and put her arm across his shoulder.

'I have lost everyone.' said Amy in a small voice.

'No my dear,' said Mrs Turner softly, 'you have Charlie and your beautiful children. Time will pass and you will see how you are blessed.'

The Turners stayed the night but left early the next morning. Mr Turner remarked that he thought his wife would stay to help clear the kitchen after the wake but she said she had left it on purpose, for there was nothing like work for occupying your mind against unhappy thoughts. He smiled to himself and urged the pony and cart forward to get them home and his wife out of the cutting wind.

The winter months were hard, though not unusually so, but they seemed to pass slowly and Amy longed for more daylight hours and some sun to cheer her. The Turners were frequent visitors for Mrs Turner was concerned for Amy's health.

'She has not rallied as I would have hoped, father,' she told her husband.

'I share your concerns and will have a word with Charlie for he is so taken up with the farm, I fear he has not noticed.'

As soon as he was able to find Charlie alone, he took him aside. 'Mrs Turner and I have noticed how lacklustre Amy is and wonder if you have noticed?'

'Aye and it is a constant concern of mine,' he replied. 'I have thought long and hard on the subject and begin to wonder if this farm has some sort of... blight. It is a good living with fine land and everything in its favour. And yet, one by one each member of this family, good and bad, has given a life for it. It will not take more while I have breath in my body, Frank,' he said shaking his head from side to side.

'What have you in mind to do?' asked Mr Turner.

'I have heard talk that the Americas have much to offer a young family. There is nothing left to keep us here... except your valued friendship of course. I think perhaps that there are too many bad memories for Amy here. You know her history as well as I. Perhaps a complete change of surroundings, a new life, will bring the colour back into her cheeks and give her a future to look forward to.'

'This is a big step to take, Charlie. How will you fund it until you find work?'

'I have a little put by and the farm should sell well. I am told that there is land to be bought cheaply over there if you put claim to it and are prepared to work to clear it and I will do anything to provide for my family. You know that, Frank.'

'Aye, Charlie. Amy and the bairns could not be in better hands. I am convinced of that. Though we shall be most sorry to see you go, I think you are doing the right thing. I, too have some money put by for a rainy day and no one to leave it to. You have been like a family to me and Mrs Turner and I would have you take it to help you on your way.' He noticed Charlie's concern. 'Don't worry yourself about us. I will see that Mrs Turner has sufficient for her needs should I leave this life first. We have had the best life together a man could hope for and I know she would wish the same for you and Amy.'

Charlie was moved to tears and the two men, one old now and the other in his prime, clung to each other in the yard for some time, unaware that their womenfolk, arms linked, viewed them from the kitchen window.

EPILOGUE

Amy did not hesitate in her agreement to Charlie's proposal. She viewed the prospect with excitement and total relief that the farm she had lived in all her life would become a thing of the past. That is not to say that there was not trepidation at a future unknown. Little was known of the Americas except that it was a land far across a vast ocean far bigger than anything they could imagine and peopled by savages and wild animals. But it was said there was good cheap land to be had and others like them with whom to build a new future for their families.

As Charlie had hoped, the farm sold well and with the few possessions intended to take with them, the family stayed a few days at the Turner's before setting out on the journey to Plymouth where they had a passage booked to a new life in a new country.

It is true that a naivety and lack of worldly knowledge made the prospect of their journey less daunting than it might have been, though one must not underestimate the brave spirit required to undertake such an endeavour when to turn back would be out of the question. Their terrible passage in tempestuous seas and the hardship they were forced to endure is another story in itself but arrive safely on America's eastern seaboard they did. It was made all the more glorious by the fact that the ground was firm beneath their feet and the life aboard ship was over. They felt that they were stronger for the experience and could face whatever life had in store for them in the future.

There is no doubt that they could not have imagined what the future did, indeed hold for them; that they were to pioneer the beginnings of a whole new nation with all the dangers and hardships, the responsibilities and power-sharing that that could involve. But the strength that can be sustained within a close and loving family is formidable indeed and in this regard, Amy and Charlie Marriot, Daisy, Little Tom and baby Frank never faltered.